# So This is Christmas

## Hart's Ridge

### Kay Bratt

# So This Is Christmas

**A Hart's Ridge Novel**

# Books by Kay Bratt

Red Skies

RED THREAD
PUBLISHING GROUP

This book is a fictional dramatization that includes one incident inspired by a real event. Facts to support that incident were drawn from a variety of sources, including published materials and interviews, then altered to fit into the fictional story. Otherwise, this book contains fictionalized scenes, composite and representative characters and dialogue, and time compression, all modified for dramatic and narrative purposes. The views and opinions expressed in the book are those of the fictional characters only and do not necessarily reflect or represent the views and opinions held by individuals on which any of the characters are based.

# Prologue

The snow outside glistened under the afternoon sun while, inside, the Colburn household was glowing with the warmth of Christmas. Jane stepped back to admire her handiwork: garlands draped along the banister, twinkling lights outlining the windows, and red bows tied to the chairs around the dining table. The stockings were hung in perfect order over the fireplace, their embroidered names a reminder of the traditions Jane and Willis had built over the years. The Christmas tree stood tall in the corner, its branches adorned with an eclectic mix of ornaments—handmade by the kids when they were little, ones passed down from their parents, and a few new ones added each year.

For the grandchildren, there were bright red-and-green presents stacked neatly under the tree, each one tied with ribbons and topped with little candy canes. The air was thick with the comforting smells of Christmas dinner—the savory aroma of roast beef, slow-cooked in Jane's secret marinade—filling the house. She'd been making it for decades now, and it was always a family favorite.

This year, she was seriously considering passing the recipe

down to Erin, her daughter-in-law. Jane smiled, thinking it might be time to start letting go of a few traditions and maybe even consider letting Seth and Erin host Christmas at their house next year.

"Willis?" Jane called out from the kitchen, her hands busy wrapping the last of the presents for the grandkids.

From his recliner in the living room, Willis gave a half-hearted groan. "Hmm?"

"Do you want to come and help me wrap these last few? I'm almost done," she asked, knowing full well what his answer would be. After more than forty years together, she could predict every word before it left his mouth.

"No way!" Willis called out, then chuckled. "I'm not missing the rest of this parade on the tube. You love that job. Why would I want to steal your joy?"

Jane rolled her eyes but laughed. He was right—she did love it. There was something so satisfying about making each package perfect, imagining the little ones tearing into the paper with their tiny, eager hands. "Alright, you've got a point. But don't think I didn't notice how you managed to dodge all the hard stuff today."

"Hey, I shoveled the walkway, didn't I?" Willis replied, raising his eyebrows in mock indignation. "Do you know how deep that snow was? Practically up to my knees. I hung those new lights up along the porch, too. So I earned this recliner time."

"Yes, I guess you did," Jane agreed, feeling a surge of affection for him. "That was a big help. Besides, you're much better at that stuff than me. Especially shoveling snow. I would've just slipped and fallen halfway to the porch."

"Exactly," Willis called out. "And we don't need any Christmas trips to the ER."

Jane laughed again as she finished wrapping the last box, a

soft hum of contentment filling her chest. It wasn't as though she didn't have to trudge through snow all the time. As a postal worker, she'd traversed in it up to her knees some winters.

Three more years and then no more delivering mail. She couldn't wait. It made the upcoming cringe of turning sixty-five a bit less, knowing that she could finally retire. She had so many plans. First thing was that she was going to take her infatuation with birds a little further and join a bird-watching club. Learn the names of all her favorites. Collect photos.

She also wanted to start her own book club. One with just her friends she'd made through her job over the years. Women like her who didn't care for dressing up and drinking wine. Ones who really wanted to share their love of reading. Get together with some tasty pick-me-ups and coffee. Learn about each other and really care about what they're reading.

"When are the kids coming again?" Willis called out.

"Seth and Erin will be here first," Jane replied, tying a bright red bow around a box. "They dropped the kids off with Erin's parents this morning, and her mom is going to bring them by right before dinner. Raya and Ronnie should be here any time now. I asked Raya to drop by early to help with peeling potatoes. She's probably finishing up something in the trailer."

"Of course she is," Willis said knowingly. Raya, their youngest daughter, lived in a mobile home on their property, just a short walk away. She had a habit of wandering over whenever the mood struck, which suited them just fine. Her new boyfriend also slowed her down a bit. As expected, he was her priority now. "And what about Missy Ann?"

Jane frowned. "She called a little while ago, and Justin has a fever. She doesn't want to bring it to us so she's skipping."

"Oh, that's too bad," Willis said. "Well, I hope they'll be alright by New Years to come for your collards and black-eyed peas. She needs to start the new year off with good luck."

3

Jane smiled, her heart swelling with that familiar warmth. Willis was always so positive. It was one of the reasons she'd married him. Christmas was his favorite time of year, too, and she loved how much he still cared about having the family together. It made all the preparations—the cooking, the cleaning, the endless wrapping—worth it.

She sure hated that Missy Ann wasn't going to make it, though. And poor Justin, to be sick on Christmas was the worst.

Jane had to admit, she couldn't wait for everyone to see their new kitchen. So far, only Raya had seen that finally, after two decades of wishing and talking about it, they'd updated the flooring and countertops and painted the cabinets. Now, instead of the dingy white tiles, her counters were warm and inviting with a few different wood tones in the butcher block style. The cabinets went from a shocking blue to a warm sage green, and her hardwood floors were in a lighter color called Alston Birch. It wasn't real hardwood, but it sure looked real. They'd put on rustic black iron cabinet and drawer pulls, and she'd decluttered in a big way. No more baskets and dusty faux plants on top of her cabinets.

All appliances except the toaster and the coffeemaker were hidden away.

Willis had also installed faux beams on the ceiling, stained to match the floors. The final touch was removing the outdated, flowered wallpaper and giving the walls a few coats of crisp white. Everything looked so clean and rustic, down to the simple wooden bowl of pinecones as her table centerpiece.

A fancy kitchen needed a fancy apron and the one she'd picked out, and was wearing now, had Santa and his elves plastered all over it. She'd picked it up the day before at Target. It was on clearance, seeing how the holiday shopping was mostly over.

She'd almost passed it by, but Raya saw her linger and urged her to buy it.

The grandkids were going to love it. Every year since her first grandbaby, she'd done just a little more to make the house festive. When she and Willis were dead and gone, she wanted them to have very vivid memories of the holidays and Papa and Nana's home.

The timer on the oven went off and she went to check the roast, peeking in and nodding her satisfaction on the golden-brown coloring. She turned the oven off but left the meat in there so that it would stay warm.

One more gift to wrap and she'd be ready. She turned the music just a tad higher because her favorite holiday song, *So This is Christmas*, by John Lennon, came on. She hurried back over to the table, admiring her new floors as she went. She couldn't stop looking. It meant even more to her that she'd gotten her dream kitchen without a complete renovation, and she loved it so much. It was so cozy, too, with the scent of the roast mingling with the sweet smell of pine and cinnamon candles she'd placed around the whole house. She could already picture the kids running through the hallways, the sound of their laughter filling the rooms, the chaotic unwrapping of gifts, and the inevitable mess that would follow. But she didn't mind. These were the years that the children were happy with any sort of toy. Time flies and it wouldn't be too long before they turned into teenagers and would probably only want money, or expensive phones and things, ruining her annual gift-buying joy and the glee of seeing them excitedly tear into the gifts.

Yes, they needed to make the most of this day. Lots of pictures, too. She needed to charge her phone, now that she'd thought about it.

She suddenly heard the familiar creak of the front door opening, and she paused in cutting through the gift wrap, waiting to hear who it was. But then, a loud, unexpected noise cut through the air—a sharp crack that echoed through the house. It was a sound she didn't immediately recognize, but it sent a chill down her spine.

*What was that noise?*

Jane's heart skipped a beat as she moved quickly toward the living room, her breath shallow. "Willis?" she called out, her voice shaky.

She rounded the corner, her feet feeling like lead as she approached the living room. The world seemed to slow down, her movements sluggish, as if she were stuck in a nightmare. And then she saw it.

The sight before her made her freeze in place, her blood running cold. She dropped the scissors she'd been holding, and they clattered loudly to the floor. Jane's mind struggled to process what she was seeing. The warmth of the holidays vanished instantly, replaced by confusion, then a chilling sense of dread.

"Willis?" she whispered, but there was no response. The air felt suffocating, and all she could hear was the pounding of her own heartbeat. Jane's world as she knew it shattered, pushing her into action. She found her feet and turned, running toward the kitchen.

# Chapter One

Taylor had never really thought about how much Cate must've loved her when she was an infant, but she did now, as she nuzzled Lennon's tiny neck. Her heart swelled with the warmth only a mother could feel, especially on as special a night as Christmas Eve. The scent of her baby—a mix of baby powder and innocence—was a balm to her frayed nerves. It had been a long journey, these three months since Lennon had arrived, and she wasn't quite the same person she'd been before. She was a mother now, and her daughter had filled a space in her heart that Taylor hadn't even known was empty. She'd also learned a valuable lesson in the last months. She wasn't invincible. Her life was just as fragile as everyone else's.

Reluctantly, she handed her baby over to Cate, though her arms ached to keep holding her. Her mother was excellent with Lennon, having birthed five of her own kids, but Taylor still fought the urge to do everything herself. Yet, the shadow of self-doubt loomed larger than she liked to admit. She wasn't quite ready to trust herself with bathing Lennon just yet.

"Come on, Tadpole," Cate cooed, effortlessly placing Lennon over her shoulder. She disappeared with her down the hall, the soft padding of her steps mixing with the distant hum of Christmas carols playing from the kitchen.

Alice was somewhere outside, most likely helping Jo and Cecil with the litter of new puppies. A stray Labrador mix and her just born litter of seven wiggly pups found in a ditch and brought to the farm the week before—their latest editions to the Walsh Wild Hearts Rescue. Too bad the pups weren't ready to go—they would've had an easy time adopting them out for that special furry gift under the tree.

The house was alive with holiday cheer, twinkling lights and the fresh, pine scent of the Christmas tree that stood tall in the corner, adorned with a patchwork of mismatched ornaments —some new, others hand-me-downs from generations past. Nothing too fancy. Her taste was one of simplicity. And things that brought about memories.

Taylor's favorite was the small angel at the top, its wings slightly crooked from years of handling. She felt a kinship with the battered figure. It had been through a lot but was still surviving from year to year. It belonged to her grandmother. Adele was living with Cate and Ellis now, having moved from Florida to Georgia recently after her beloved little dog died.

It took some talking, but they'd all convinced her that they wanted her there where she could be near her family for her late years. With Cate and Ellis' help, she'd rid herself of most of her home's belongings, other than sentimental objects that she handed out to family members, saying she didn't need them anymore.

Her property had gone up in value substantially over the years, and the proceeds had landed her a nice nest egg. They'd encouraged her to spend it doing something like travel, or for a new car, but Adele waved all their suggestions away, saying she'd never been a frivolous person and she sure as the dickens wasn't going to start now.

Adele was loving having a new purpose now and as far as Anna was concerned, was instrumental in keeping all the clients for the Gray Escape Bed & Biscuit in line. The pets were never the problem—it was their people who couldn't follow rules. Some picked up late, were no shows, or complained if their little Fido was found with a speck of dirt between their paws.

But Adele didn't take any flak and soon, the customers were realizing that the business was successful enough to turn them away if needed and make them find somewhere else for their pets to stay while they were away.

And none of them wanted that.

The Gray's boarding business was the most in demand in the county.

Using Diesel's new harness for support, Taylor carefully got to her feet, the feel of the floor beneath her still unfamiliar after so many weeks confined to bed and wheelchair. She went to the window, where Sam was outside, bundled in a thick jacket, his breath visible in the frosty air as he worked on an engine for Lila's Lexus. She was one of his best-paying clients and needed it for the next day—and was willing to pay double.

Sam's hands moved with expert precision, but Taylor knew him well enough to catch the tension in his shoulders. Yes, it was Christmas, and he shouldn't be working, but they needed the money, and, with her only getting a partial paycheck from work now, every little bit counted. Cate had tried to keep her on the payroll of the family dog boarding business, but Taylor wasn't going to take money for doing nothing.

She sighed, the cool glass of the window offering little comfort. The sheriff had been kind enough to push her paperwork through without too much trouble or probing, ensuring she was covered under the county's disability policy. It was only fair —after all, she'd contracted fungal meningitis on the job. But the sixty percent pay didn't stretch as far as they needed, not with the baby and her medical bills stacking up. And though she was grateful to be on her feet again, she still spent a lot of the day feeling weak and unreliable. She could walk now, yes, but only short distances, and standing for too long felt like running a marathon. A walker was helpful around the house, but, even with that, her arms gave out quickly.

Her gaze shifted back to the living room, where the decorations were set for tonight's family dinner. The table was covered in a deep red cloth, the edges trimmed with gold embroidery. Plates were already set—dainty flowered China her mother had insisted on using—while candles in brass holders flickered gently. The smells of rosemary, cinnamon, and roasting turkey wafted from the kitchen, filling the house with a cozy, festive aroma. It was the first Christmas she hadn't been up and doing a lot of the holiday prep herself. Instead, she was the one being fussed over.

Attention-getter was not her favorite role. She'd always focused on seeking respect. It lasted longer than attention. Her phone buzzed on the side table, but she ignored it. Jo had texted earlier, reminding her to "breathe through it" if things got overwhelming.

Her ongoing therapy was supposed to help her process emotions, especially the big ones she'd buried while battling her illness and then through the first weeks of having Lennon in her arms. Soon though, the unease had emerged, then settled and had nearly paralyzed her. But with intense therapy, she was now learning to accept that anxiety was part of her life now.

But old habits die hard.

Sometimes, even now, the struggle of it all threatened to pull her under like quicksand.

But Jo and her therapist's words were getting through, and Taylor was working on it. Slowly, surely, she was learning how to feel without letting the emotions consume her. Her anxiety coach had introduced her to techniques she never would have imagined trying before—meditation, breathwork, body tapping.

Stuff that had once seemed too abstract now felt necessary.

Now she was learning how much stress could wreak havoc on her already fragile body, and if she had any hope of fully recovering—of being the mother Lennon and Alice needed and the wife that Sam deserved—she had to get control of it.

The Christmas lights blinked rhythmically, and Taylor felt a small smile tug at her lips. She was here. Home. With Sam. With Lennon and Alice.

That was a blessing, wasn't it?

Diesel, ever the guardian, nudged her leg gently, sensing her distraction. His new harness made standing and moving easier, and she was grateful for his unflinching loyalty. He had been her rock during those long days in the hospital, lying beside her bed, steady and patient.

She rested a hand on his head, feeling the comforting warmth of his presence.

Cate returned, her face lit up in that serene glow she always wore when holding her grandchildren. "She's down for a nap," she said softly. "And before you say anything, yes, I sang her that silly lullaby you like." She winked at Taylor and moved toward the kitchen, humming to herself as she checked on dinner.

Taylor felt the exhaustion creeping in again. Standing too long drained her, but there was a peacefulness in the air tonight, a calm she hadn't felt in what seemed like forever. She moved back to the couch, lowering herself slowly, and let the warmth of the room envelop her.

Sam came inside just as Cate pulled the turkey from the oven, his cheeks red from the cold. He shook the snow off his boots and looked over at Taylor, his eyes softening the moment they met hers. "How are you doing, babe?" he asked, coming over and kneeling beside her. His hand—rough from the day's work but so familiar, so comforting—found hers.

"I'm good," she whispered. "Tired, but good."

Sam kissed her forehead. "You should rest more," he said, always the worrier. But his smile told her he knew she wouldn't.

Taylor had never been good at sitting still.

Dinner was almost ready, the smells now filling every corner of the house. Cecil, Ellis, and her sisters would be here soon, with kids in tow. Corbin and Sutton weren't going to make it, as they were stuck in traffic coming from Nashville, where Corbin had put on a small concert. He was slowly taking on more public venues and they missed seeing him around the farm so much.

For a moment, Taylor let herself soak in the feeling of normalcy. Ignoring the faint pleading within her to get back to her job. To serving the people of Hart's Ridge. To protecting those she'd pledged to protect. She'd never known a time when she wasn't busy doing. Outside, snow began to fall, soft flakes drifting lazily from the sky. Christmas lights blinked from the porch and surrounding trees. Inside, Taylor finally felt a sense of peace she hadn't known she needed. Tonight wasn't about presents or decorations. It was about being here, together, for Lennon's first Christmas. And, for now, that was more than enough.

# Chapter Two

**D**o what you can with what you have and where you are. That was Taylor's mantra for the day as she moved around the dining room, distractedly adjusting silverware, filling glasses with sweet tea or water, and basically trying to make herself useful. She wanted everyone to stop treating her like a patient. The house hummed with warmth and laughter as everyone began arriving for dinner—all except Lucy and Johnny. Taylor had already checked her phone twice in the last ten minutes, hoping to see a message from her sister explaining the delay, but the screen remained dark and empty. The others noticed, too; Cate and the other sisters had already sent their own texts, which went unanswered.

Cate came in and placed a reassuring hand on Taylor's shoulder. "I'm sure she just got held up at the gallery," she said, more to reassure herself than anyone else.

"Yeah, you're probably right. Let's go ahead with dinner." She hoped Lucy would arrive eventually, maybe juggling last-minute sales or an eager client.

Just as they began filling plates, a knock sounded at the door. Sam, ever the gracious host, put down his napkin and went to answer it. Taylor could hear him exchange a quiet word with someone before he stepped aside, letting in a slight figure—a young woman, barely more than a girl. Pale as the moonlight with hair like soft wheat falling around her shoulders. A teardrop tattoo was inked delicately beside one eye with a fresh bandage covering her other eyebrow. She looked misplaced, uncertain, as her eyes flitted from face to face in the room.

Taylor's heart leapt. "Quig?" Her voice broke through the murmurs of confusion as she took a step forward, seeing her friend who had been by her side in ways most people would never understand.

Quig's face lit up, and, before either of them could say another word, she crossed the room in a few quick strides and wrapped her arms around Taylor.

The world fell away for a moment as they clung to each other, tears slipping from their eyes, born from a place deeper than mere friendship—a bond forged in desperation and survival.

Taylor finally pulled back, introducing her. "This is Quig," she said, smiling through her tears. "Remember, the girl who saved my life? Broke a window with a chair to get the CO's attention. If she hadn't, I might not be here."

Quig flushed, clearly embarrassed by the praise. "Aw, it wasn't like that. I just did what anyone would've done," she mumbled, looking down. "The other girls helped, too."

Sam stepped forward, his expression solemn as he extended a hand. "Well, thank you for saving my wife. We'll never forget what you did."

Quig managed a shy smile and then her gaze fell on little Lennon, gurgling in Cate's arms. "Oh, there she is. Can I ... can I hold her?" she asked, her voice tentative, as if afraid her rough past would disqualify her from touching an infant.

Taylor nodded, and watched as Quig took Lennon with

surprising tenderness, settling with her in the chair and rocking her gently. She saw in Quig's touch a kind of practiced gentleness that hinted at a mother's heart.

Lennon, mesmerized by Quig's big blue eyes in her shockingly pale face, lay content and still in her arms. Taylor's throat tightened as she noticed the bandage hiding the tattoo on Quig's eyebrow, the one that had once read "Fate." She wondered if covering it was a way of letting go of all the pain Quig had endured, of all the past mistakes she wanted to bury.

Anna and Jo started a squabble about the green beans and how Jo had wanted to add butter, but Anna refused, had claimed it was too fattening.

Quig heard them, too, and she raised her eyebrows at Taylor. There was a sudden banging of a fork against a plate, an angry retort, then silence between them.

"Not uncommon," Taylor whispered. "Anna is our Kitchen Queen, and Jo gets tired of her being bossy. It'll blow over."

She hoped so, anyway. She was too tired to get involved.

Back in the day, the argument would've gone on for hours, maybe days. Sisters taking their deep, buried frustrations at their dismal life out with petty spats over nothing. Taylor had played referee their whole childhood, though, she had to admit, it was usually Lucy as the main player. Jo was so laid back that she normally just shrugged and walked away when something came up. But Jo had been through a lot, and, like she'd always done, was holding the hurt and betrayal so deep that no one could talk to her about it.

It was surprising that this was the first squabble of the day. In a family of four sisters, one of them was always irritating another.

So an argument over butter made perfect sense.

"Well, how about them Braves," Cecil said cheerfully, causing a chuckle to move around the room. With that, dinner progressed, everyone sharing stories and laughter around the table. Taylor noted how Quig stayed close to Lennon, holding the baby's hand and making silly faces that had the little one cooing with delight.

Cate laughed aloud about something that Ellis whispered in her ear. The room buzzed with warmth, everyone teasing and swapping stories, each tale more ridiculous than the last.

Even though it wasn't Thanksgiving, her grandmother had made pumpkin pie, and she got up, went to the kitchen for it, and returned and set it on the table.

When Taylor's dad tried to cut him a piece, it oozed out of pie form and puddled in the dish.

"Adele, what do we have here? Boneless pie?"

She glared at him. "I guess it didn't set properly, you ass."

Everyone laughed and she finally smiled. It was no secret that they weren't fans of each other, but at least now they could sit at the same dinner table.

"I brought a lemon meringue pie from Walmart," Jo said. "I'll go dish it up. C'mon, Levi, you can help me."

Levi groaned but followed her to the kitchen.

Cate finally leaned over toward Taylor, asking softly about Caleb and Lydia.

Taylor's face softened. "Last I heard, they were somewhere around the Grand Tetons," she said, picturing the small family driving around the mountains, far from the gossip and whispers that had clouded their lives since Lydia's ordeal. They all agreed that leaving his job was a good choice for Caleb, a chance to spend a final year all together, recovering their sense of peace before his eldest headed off to college—a healing journey, just the five of them in a comfortable RV, wrapped in nature and each other's presence.

She didn't mention that part of their trip would be to deliver Shara Williams' ashes to her family. Turned out that Norman

Addler's mother was also an abducted victim, snatched away when she was still in college and lived decades too afraid to contact her loved ones. It was important for Lydia to find anyone left of Shara's family and let them know that she was finally at peace.

"Where's the dressing?" Jackson said loudly. "I hope Cate made it. Hers is the best I've ever had."

Cate blushed but passed the dish.

Her dad hadn't brought anyone with him to dinner, and lately hadn't said anything about his relationship status. They assumed that the girlfriend he was so serious about was over now. Taylor was relieved that his presence didn't bother Ellis in any way. It wasn't usual to have to eat Christmas dinner with your wife's ex-husband, but he took it well. In some homes, it would be enough to spark a visit from the local authorities, and sometimes the conflicts could get really bad. Celebrations seemed to bring out family dramas that had been simmering all year long.

So much for holiday spirit. She wondered who got the short straw and was on Christmas Eve shift at the department, then tried to divert her thoughts. Shane had probably volunteered, but that was the last thing she needed to be worried about right now.

Platters of food circled the table, hands passing mashed potatoes and sharing bowls of steaming gravy and buttered rolls. Taylor noticed how Cate and Ellis exchanged soft glances and lingering touches, their love like a gentle current running beneath the joyful chaos of the gathering.

Adele looked on, a ghost of her old stubbornness flickering in her eyes, but there was a new fragility there, too, a gentleness brought on by loss and change. Moving from Florida, losing her beloved dog—it had all softened her in ways Taylor hadn't expected. She reached across the table and squeezed Adele's hand.

Adele looked up and smiled softly. "It's a good day," she said.

"Yes, it is," Taylor agreed. She waved Quig to the table to take a chair, which she did tentatively after placing Lennon in her bouncy seat.

The food was great, as usual. Along with turkey, there was ham. Anna had baked the ham and taken care of the majority of the main dishes. Jo had gone over to help her cook the day before. The fact that Anna had not fussed when they had to carry it all to Taylor's house was a miracle, but it seemed that, along with the joy she was gaining from her nursing classes, she was becoming an easier person all around. Except when it came to green beans and butter, it seemed.

Taylor had to admit, she enjoyed being with Anna now, a complete change from how it used to be like walking on glass. Anna was softer, more empathetic. Taylor was also suspicious that Anna was finally talking to someone romantically, too. Her sister hadn't admitted as much, but there were signs.

She'd tell it when she wanted to. Taylor wouldn't push, she just hoped Anna was choosing carefully. The Gray girls had a lot of bad luck when it came to men. Except for Sam. He'd broken the streak of her trail of tears.

"I have an announcement," Ellis said, and everyone quieted. "Guess who is going to Mexico this summer?"

Jackson raised his hand, and Ellis laughed.

"My daughter is getting married, and the wedding is in Cabo," he said. "Cate and I will be attending and staying at an all-inclusive resort."

There were cheers, and Cate smiled shyly, meeting Taylor's eyes across the table.

Of course, her mother would be gracious about it, but Cate

felt very self-conscious around Ellis' kids. Yes, they claimed to accept her now, but there was still an awkward air between them.

"Doesn't your son live on Maui?" Cecil asked.

Ellis nodded, then chuckled. "He sure does. He's already bellyaching about how far he has to travel. He's trying to get his sister to pay for accommodations because of it."

Taylor wondered if any of the rest of her family would be invited. Ellis' daughter had been to the farm a few times, and they'd gotten to know her a bit more. She'd even brought her fiancé to a cookout the summer before. He was a nice guy from a modest upbringing that was much different than the upscale life Ellis had given his children. From Taylor's view, the fiancé fit better in with the Grays, though he looked eager to make his fiancée a happy woman.

She hoped he didn't have to try too hard and that he could be confident in who he truly was, without feeling the need to keep his humble beginnings close to his chest.

When dessert was finally served, the children gobbled it up and raced for the door, so eager to see the new puppies that they didn't even demand to open the gifts around the tree. They were doing a grab bag exchange this year. Ten-dollar limit and anything went. Should make for some laughs. But it was forgotten in the more attractive allure of puppy kisses.

Alice and Levi ran off the porch neck and neck, while Teague sprinted ahead with a triumphant whoop, Bronwyn trailing behind with a pout.

Taylor chuckled. "Diesel," she called out.

He came running out from under the table where he and Brandy, Cate's dog, had been searching for crumbs. Taylor pointed at the kids headed toward the barn.

"Go with them."

Diesel didn't need to be told twice. He raced after the children obediently, always ready to join the pack that he was so fond of. Taylor knew he'd come back to alert her to any emergencies faster than a kid's legs could run. She could relax when he was with them.

Brandy settled next to Cate's legs. The loyal dog never left her mother's side.

"C'mon, Jo," Anna said. "Let's clear the table. Mom said she and Ellis will do the dishes. They like to cozy up elbow to elbow." She made a sarcastic face.

"I'll help, too," Taylor said. "I'm not an invalid."

Still yet, she was much slower than they were and only carried one thing at a time.

When everything was cleared, Taylor and Quig found a few quiet minutes to slip out onto the porch. They stood in the cool evening air, shoulders brushing, the sounds of Jo and the others laughing as they tidied up drifting through the open window.

Quig spoke first, her voice low. "I've got a new job."

"Oh, that's fantastic. What is it?"

"A warehouse. Nothing fancy," Quig said quietly. "It's hard to get a good job when you're a felon. But I've started attending narcotics anonymous meetings, too. I'm forty-six days sober."

Taylor felt a swell of pride for her friend and told her so, only to hear about the rough living situation—a couch offered by an old boss, the bridges burnt with her own family. The girl was so smart and could do a lot better than a warehouse job and a couch to sleep on.

"You might not see it right now, but you're doing amazing," Taylor said, her voice warm. She watched Quig's face soften, a spark of hope flickering in her eyes.

Quig glanced down, her hands fidgeting. "Thanks. And thanks for inviting me today. I wasn't going to come but changed my mind at the last minute."

"I'm glad you did," Taylor said.

"When I found out you were an undercover, I was ... mad. But after a while, I realized it was different. You saw the good in me before I even saw it myself." She looked up, her face open and vulnerable. "It made me wanna try, to really try. And I'm grateful, Taylor. You were a friend when I didn't deserve one."

"I'm glad I could at least be that."

"Oh, Pikachu was demoted, and Deputy Freeman was fired. The girls were inspired by you, and he had multiple reports about his inappropriate touching. Word has it that the sheriff and captain pulled a lot of video footage over the last months to verify it, and they gave him the axe to make an example of him to the other guards."

Taylor smiled, feeling a bit of victory, though getting rid of one or two bad guards wasn't going to stop the next ones from coming in. She and Quig shared a quiet moment.

"What about Lyric?" Taylor asked.

"She got her sentence finally, but she's doing okay, because of you. She's working on more art projects and is still hoping to get into an art school when she gets out."

Quig's words made Taylor blush, and she waved off the compliment, humbled by the impact her presence had left. Once she'd stabled in the hospital, she'd thought that she'd failed her assignment, but turns out that it was much more than just giving ideas on how to improve the women's pods. Yes, the sheriff over there had some issues to address—things like drugs coming in under trays and other things she'd witnessed. But, in her opinion, the most important issues were those that affected the mental health of the inmates. They needed more structure. Health care. Classes and books. The inmates needed to have avenues to improve themselves while incarcerated, the re-offend rate could possibly go way down. Taylor thought he also needed a big shakedown in his personnel to get rid of those in uniform who couldn't find any compassion or respect for the unfortunates who ended up under their control. Everything didn't have to be a power struggle, and empathy could go a long way into keeping the pods peaceful.

She and Quig were deep in conversation about some of the girls there when Taylor's phone buzzed in her pocket. She pulled it out, reading the name on the screen with surprise. Shane. Her heart pounded as she opened the message.

> Just a heads up, we've got a quadruple murder in town.

The porch and Quig's soft laughter faded into the background as Taylor stared at the message, the words settling in her mind.

Her first thought was who was it? Who had they lost? Faces fanned through her mind, smiles of those around town that she'd come to care for, and protect.

Who would she never see smiling again?

When she glanced up, she saw Sam was watching her from the doorway, his brow knitted in worry as he crossed his arms over his chest. He shook his head slowly, as if sensing that something big was pulling her back in and he needed to remind her that, for now, her focus had to be on herself and Lennon, not on protecting the people of Hart's Ridge.

# Chapter Three

Shane couldn't remember where he'd read it, but a saying was going round and round in his mind: *"Dread it, run from it, but destiny arrives all the same."* He squinted into the dim afternoon light as he pulled up to 818 Beaver Trail Road. A rusted farm gate stood open, the dirt road beyond it stretching out before him like a path leading to hell. Deputy Kuno was there guarding the entrance and stood aside, letting him through.

Shane eased his truck down the road, gravel crunching under his tires, and braced himself mentally for the scene ahead. He wished so badly that Taylor was in the seat next to him. The last few months without her by his side had been torture. She was only a deputy, but, if he was being honest, she was probably an even better detective than he was. It was something about her sense of selflessness that gave her that extra edge on putting the pieces together. It was something she'd been born with. Since high school, Taylor had been rescuing anyone or anything that came into her path, pushing her own needs beneath the surface.

The fact that she'd almost died because she was too stubborn to see to her own health hadn't sat well with him, and he hoped that it had been enough to really make her think and realize that she had issues.

She wasn't fooling him. He was no professional, but he had it already figured out. The way that Taylor was wired was because of some kind of crazy, unacknowledged need to heal her own wounds. She gave the care and attention to others that she couldn't give to herself—or even accept for herself—that for whatever reason, she didn't think she's deserving of.

It was pure bullshit the way they all took advantage of her. Her family always pulling on her for this or that. Keeping her dad alive. Keeping Lucy out of trouble. Catering to Anna's needs. Even Sam expecting her to take on his kid who had her own issues—that one really took the cake. And now a baby when she wasn't even recovered from the crap that landed her in the hospital in critical care. It really pissed him off.

He glanced at his phone. Mira had tried to call a few times. He was going to have to explain to her that, just like if she was leading a search, he wasn't going to be available until it simmered down a bit. She was a lot like Taylor in that she was completely dedicated to her career, but she was harder.

Taylor tried to act tough, but deep down she didn't have a mean bone in her body. She was soft, malleable.

He took the curve too fast and threw up gravel trying to slow down. His imagination created a picture of Taylor sitting in the rocking chair, her new baby against her chest. He'd met Lennon on her one-month birthday, and she was probably the most beautiful baby he'd ever seen. A mix of her dad's blonde features but with Taylor's deep brown eyes. Eyes that seemed to look deep into your soul with an intensity that locked you in.

Someone needed to step in and take all Taylor's responsibilities up. Let her heal so that she could come back to work, where she wanted to be, in his opinion. He didn't care what Sam said—he'd only been in the picture a few years.

Shane had known Taylor nearly all her life. Like, *really* knew her.

Taylor would never accept any of his psychobabble, even if he was brave enough to try to point it out. No, their relationship worked well because they didn't go deep. He wasn't going to screw that up. But, hell, he missed her. Especially now, with a homicide case in his lap.

He pulled up in front of the house. Before he could even get out of his truck, he heard the sheriff's truck screech to a halt behind him.

Sheriff Dawkins stepped out, his face as stony as ever, but his mouth was a grim line as he took in the quiet horror that awaited them. Shane met him in front of the porch, giving a quick nod to Deputy Gonzalez, who was already setting up yellow tape and ordering the few deputies on site to secure the perimeter.

"What do we know?" Sheriff Dawkins asked, his voice clipped. He motioned to another deputy, barking at him to keep everyone clear. Despite Dawkins' attempt to hold his composure, Shane could see the flicker of dread in his eyes.

Shane scanned his notes on his phone, his voice low. "Nancy Hurst came by half an hour ago to drop off her two grandkids. No one came to the door, so she peeked in and saw blood on the floor. She called it in, and dispatch sent Gonzalez over for a welfare check. He saw the blood himself and kicked down the door. Found two bodies inside and two more out back in the shed. All four cold and starting to stiffen."

The sheriff cursed under his breath, his jaw tightening. "They go to church with us. Willis and I go fishing at least once or twice a summer. Is it them?"

Shane nodded, feeling sorry for Dawkins. "Yep. Nancy

Hurst identified them at the shed. The other two ... are their adult son and his wife. Hurst's daughter. She's in pieces."

Right on cue, a shrill, keening wail pierced the stillness, shattering whatever calm they had left. They turned to see Nancy Hurst, her face a mask of anguish, being led into the back seat of a patrol car by Deputy Gonzalez. The young officer looked pale, barely holding himself together—probably his first time at a scene like this. He hadn't been with them but about two months, hired as a replacement for Grimes. Hell of a way to break in a new man.

He approached them.

"Where're the kids?" Sheriff Dawkins asked, his eyes darting toward the patrol car that held the Hurst woman, her cries still audible, clearly devastated at what she'd found.

Shane pointed toward a white van parked a little way off. "They're in there with Wesley Wright from Family Services. Got a counselor on the way. The kids haven't seen anything. Haven't been told anything either, far as we know."

The sheriff's face softened, though his eyes remained troubled. "What a shit show. Two innocent kids lose their whole family on Christmas. Life doesn't get much crueler."

When no one replied, Dawkins turned to Gonzalez. "Gilmore County Sheriff is sending some of his deputies over. I want a door-to-door canvassing, and every home checked, in case our suspect is hiding out."

"The homes around here are pretty spread out," Gonzalez said.

"I don't care if they're a hundred miles apart, just do what I told you to do." Dawkins looked like he was about to have a stroke. "Search the fields, hills, and trees between, too."

"Yes, sir," Gonzalez said, nodding hard as he scurried off.

Shane drew in a steadying breath, then motioned for the sheriff to follow him inside. The house smelled of pine and something delicious cooking, an eerie contrast to the scene that lay within. He stepped carefully past the forensic team, who were setting up cameras and collecting evidence in grim silence. They'd made it in record time, coming from Jasper.

He and the sheriff moved into the living room, where Seth Colburn lay face up on the floor, his head and neck marred with bullet wounds. His eyes were open, staring up at the ceiling as if still in shock. Shane felt his stomach tighten but forced himself to remain detached, to look at the scene with a trained eye instead of the revulsion he felt creeping in.

There was a gun rack hanging over the fireplace, heavy with a few long guns. Shane went to it and examined, noting the thick layer of dust on tops of the firearms. The guns wouldn't have been used in the killings. They obviously hadn't been touched for ages.

They walked through the bedrooms, stopping in the primary. The bed was made up neatly, a cozy quilt that looked like something his mom would make. He went to a nightstand, opened it and found a semi-automatic 380 pistol and a Walther Kurz 9 mm. They were loaded but did not have rounds in the chamber. A box of 38 caliber bullets was deeper in the drawer.

In the kitchen, they found Erin, wife of Seth Colburn. She was curled up, wedged between the fridge and the wall, knees pulled to her chest, her face barely recognizable. Shane swallowed hard, picturing the fear she must have felt—seeing her husband murdered, running away, only to meet the same fate. The scene painted in his mind was one of complete terror.

"Looks like she tried to hide when she realized she was cornered," he murmured to Dawkins, nodding toward the living room.

They went back out and around to the back of the house and walked over to the shed where a handful of more forensic officers were working. No one was touching the bodies yet and

Shane was glad for that. He had to take his own set of photos, too.

On the ramp leading up to the shed door was a huge bundle with a man's boot sticking out of it. Someone had placed a big rolled carpet on top of the body in a clumsy attempt to hide it.

"I'm assuming they couldn't get Willis inside," Sheriff said. "He's a big fellow."

Shane nodded.

They could see inside and had a direct view of Jane Colburn, her body at an awkward angle as though someone just threw her inside and didn't try to move her again. Her left elbow rested against an antique-looking, red gasoline can, and her feet lay atop a grass bagger that was attached to the riding lawn-mower next to her.

The sheriff's face was hard, but his eyes flickered with sorrow. "Damn it all. They were good people. Just going about their lives ..."

Shane's phone buzzed, a sharp break in the silence. He checked the message, then looked up at Dawkins. "Their youngest daughter, Raya, just got here. Kuno stopped them at the gate."

The sheriff straightened, squaring his shoulders. "Let's go talk to her."

They headed that way. The late afternoon sun was slipping behind the trees, casting long shadows across the property as they walked down the driveway, then the dirt road, and approached a black truck idling near the gate.

Kuno stood near it, too, with his German Shepherd at his side. The dog had gone through training and got casual clearance to accompany Kuno on patrol. He wouldn't be let anywhere near the crime scene, but he looked content sitting and waiting at his master's side.

Inside the truck sat Raya Colburn, eyes wide and hollow, her face pale, surrounded by her long, brown hair.

A bearded man sat in the passenger seat, his hand resting protectively on her knee.

Dawkins approached his side, requesting identification through the passenger window.

"Name, please?"

"Ronnie McGill," he replied, slipping his ID out of his wallet and handing it over. "What's going on?"

Shane circled around to Raya's side, motioning for her to roll down the window. She looked up, her gaze flicking nervously between him and the sheriff.

"Ms. Colburn, there's an investigation in progress," Shane said gently, but firmly. He watched her reaction, looking for any hint of understanding or alarm.

Raya's brow furrowed. "Did something happen ... down at the Wilson's place?"

Shane shook his head, his voice grave. "No, it's at your parents' home. Where were you today?"

When she didn't answer, Ronnie leaned over, responding for her. "Hi. I'm her fiancé. We were headed to Vegas. Planned to get married today but we had an issue with the truck running hot, then the engine light came on, so we decided to turn around. I was going to have Willis take a look under the hood."

Shane exchanged a quick look with the sheriff, who nodded back.

"Ms. Colburn, I'd like to ask you some questions about your family," Shane said, nodding at Dawkins to stay with Ronnie. "If you'd come with me to a cruiser over here, please."

Raya hesitated, glancing toward Ronnie, but she followed Shane, climbing out of her truck and trailing behind him to Kuno's cruiser. She slipped into the passenger seat of the vehicle. Shane observed her carefully, noting the strained look on her face. He'd seen shock look a hundred different ways—and she appeared to be one of those who slipped into a calm, silent state. He always found those easier to deal with than the ones who were hysterical.

He'd have to take his turn with Nancy Hurst soon.

Shane sat down, glanced out the window at the growing police presence, then turned back to Raya. "Before we start, I need to let you know I'll be recording our conversation." He set his phone on the console and hit the record button.

She nodded silently, folding her hands in her lap. "Is ... is someone stealing cars again?" she asked, almost as if she were trying to piece together a reason for all this chaos. "Did they take my Camaro?"

Shane's heart sank. "No, this isn't about a stolen vehicle." He paused, watching her closely. This was the hardest part, and he hated it every time. "Your parents were found murdered on the property."

Raya looked past him, her eyes distant, staring out the window as if she hadn't heard him or couldn't comprehend what he was saying. Shane considered pressing her but decided to give her a moment to process and work through the instant shock.

"I know this is difficult," he said softly, his voice gentle.

She turned to him, her eyes blank.

"But how? Why?" she finally said, her voice barely audible.

"That's what we're going to find out. And I need to ask you some questions to help me understand what happened."

Raya nodded, still staring into the distance. "Okay."

"Let's start with this. Do you know anyone who'd want to hurt your parents?" he asked.

She shook her head, a tiny movement. "No ... I mean, they got along with everyone, as far as I know."

"Do you have other siblings?"

"An older sister in Atlanta, and a brother who lives nearby," she replied, her voice barely above a whisper.

"When was the last time you saw your parents?" Shane asked, trying to read her expression. He wasn't ready to tell her about her brother, yet.

"I went shopping with my mom yesterday. She let me pick out movies at Target for my Christmas gift. Ronnie and I collect them."

"What about your brother? When did you see him last?"

She shrugged. "It's been a while. He's always busy with his wife and kids. We were all supposed to have dinner together today, if I hadn't decided to go get married."

She stopped talking, lowering her head.

"Well, can you narrow down when you think you saw him last?"

"I guess on Thanksgiving," she said.

"Okay. Good. Now, when did you leave for Vegas?"

"Last night," she murmured.

"And you haven't been back until now?"

She nodded.

"I'm sorry to tell you, Raya, but your brother and his wife were also found deceased."

Raya turned her gaze to the window, watching the deputies as they moved around the property, her face hidden. Shane didn't have siblings, but he could only imagine what it would feel like if he did, and someone told him they, along with his parents, were gone. All in one stroke.

"I know this is a lot to process, but I'm going to need you to come down to the station for an official statement," he said, glancing over at her. "But for now, let's go back to your fiancé. I have to take some photos of you both, and then you can go home. I'm sorry, but you won't be able to go to where your parents and brother are, as it's a restricted crime scene."

"Oh—okay. What do you need photos for?"

"It's just routine in a case like this," he said.

As Raya climbed out of the truck, Shane's phone buzzed again. It was probably Mira, wondering what time he was picking her up for pizza. He wouldn't be picking her up at all.

He looked down, reading the incoming text. It wasn't Mira.

It was a brief message from Taylor, a small lifeline in the middle of the darkness that surrounded him now. A reminder that he was right, he knew her better than anyone.

> Tell me how I can help. Please. Don't leave me out of this.

**\* \* \***

Shane approached Nancy Hurst, who stood by her car, clutching her coat tight around her shoulders as if it could shield her from the surreal and horrific scene that was now her reality. Her face was pale, the lines of age and worry deepened, and her eyes, red-rimmed and swollen, held a hollow sort of grief that Shane had seen too many times.

Sometimes he hated his job.

He took a steadying breath and softened his voice, showed her his badge that hung on a lanyard around his neck.

"Mrs. Hurst," he said gently, "I'm Detective Weaver, can you tell me how you came to have the kids today?"

Nancy blinked, her gaze dropping to her hands, which trembled slightly as she wrung them together. "Jane and I both wanted them for Christmas Eve," she explained, her voice a strained whisper. "We agreed I'd take them last night so they could stay over and have breakfast, then open their gifts. Then I'd bring them over here for a late lunch, so they could spend the rest of the day here and open more presents. I just ... I just wanted them to have a good Christmas."

She paused, her face crumpling.

He waited, giving her the space to gather herself.

She swallowed, took a shaky breath, and went on. "When we got here, I knocked, but no one answered. I thought maybe they were just in the back or busy, or maybe down at Raya's trailer ... but there was no answer there either. I tried calling Erin ... it went straight to voicemail." Her eyes filled with tears, and she shook her head. "I—I had this awful feeling. I can't explain it. So I drove back up to the house."

Shane nodded, his voice calm. "What did you do when you got back here?"

"I don't know why but something told me to tell the kids to stay in the car." Her voice broke, and she swiped at her cheeks. She fell silent, a shudder running through her, and Shane waited, allowing her the silence to process the memory. Her gaze was distant, fixed somewhere beyond the present, back in that moment of dread and fear. "I went up to the door and knocked again. Then I tried the handle, but it was locked," she said, her voice barely a whisper. "So I walked around, tried to look through the window ... and that's when I saw ... I couldn't tell what it was at first. But there was ... there was something on the floor. It looked like blood."

She choked on the last word, her hands trembling harder now. "I ... I panicked. Called 911. I knew something was wrong. I knew it."

Shane felt a knot form in his chest. Scenes like this one never got easier. "And after that? Did you ... look anywhere else around the property?"

Nancy shook her head. "Not by myself, but when the deputy came, I ... after we found Jane and Willis, I followed him inside, and that's when we ... when we found Erin and Seth."

Her voice broke completely, and she let out a sound—a keening, heart-wrenching sob that seemed to tear through the quiet. "My poor Erin ..." She pressed her hands to her mouth, shoulders shaking as the sobs poured out of her, each one more anguished than the last.

Shane felt rooted to the spot, unsure of what to do, the usual words of comfort catching in his throat. He raised a hand, hovering it over her shoulder for a moment before finally placing it there, a small gesture of support that felt so woefully inadequate.

"Nancy," he said softly, waiting until she looked up at him, her tear-streaked face a portrait of grief. "Are you planning to take the children home with you once Wesley gives the okay?"

She sniffled, wiping her cheeks with the back of her hand. "Do you ... do you think he'll let me?"

Shane offered a small nod. "I don't see why not. Especially since you kept them from ... from seeing anything inside." He hesitated, then asked gently, "Do you have someone who can help you break the news to them?"

Nancy's face crumpled again as fresh tears spilled down her cheeks. "How am I going to tell them, Shane? How am I supposed to tell those babies they ... they'll never see their parents again?" Her voice cracked, and the agony in her eyes was like a punch to his gut.

"We can arrange for a counselor to help with that," he assured her. "Why don't you go over to the van, check on them? See if they need you."

Nancy nodded, her movements slow and deliberate, as if the weight of the world was pressing down on her. She took a shaky breath, glanced at Shane one last time, then turned and made her way to the waiting van, where the children sat, blissfully unaware of the tragedy that had shattered their world.

Shane watched her go, a feeling of helplessness washing

over him. Two young lives, forever altered, marred by a loss they couldn't yet comprehend. They would never have a normal Christmas again. He clenched his jaw, a wave of empathy and anger swirling within him. The image of Nancy's haunted face stayed with him, a reminder of the ripple effect of violence and the devastation left in its wake.

He squared his shoulders, steeling himself against the sorrow, and turned back toward the house. There was still work to be done. But as he moved forward, he couldn't shake the nagging thought that the hardest part of this case—the lives shattered, the grief laid bare—was only just beginning.

*The Avengers.*

That was where the quote had come from.

"Dread it, run from it, but destiny arrives all the same." That was his thought as he climbed the porch to return to the brutal crime scene that awaited.

# Chapter Four

They say that certainty is the calm before the storm, but Taylor was feeling anything but confident as she carefully peeled the gift wrap away from the handle of what was obviously a cane. She already had a few, but, as she got the last of it off, she saw that this one had a built-in flashlight.

"Thank you," she said as Alice and Sam beamed, waiting on her approval.

It was a nice gesture, but she wanted to be done with canes, walkers, and, of course, the wheelchair. She didn't need to start a collection. The sooner she could get back to full, physical abilities, the better. She'd spent the day avoiding the chair, and now she was paying for it. Her body was aching and weak, and her mind was on bedtime. She hoped it would be an easy night getting Lennon to sleep. As much as she loved their ritual of being in the rocking chair together, Taylor singing lullabies and then whispering into her ear until she drifted off to sleep.

The next gift was better. It was the rubber boots she'd seen at Tractor Supply and admired. She called them muck boots and they all wore them around the kennels and other places on the farm. It was an unspoken challenge with all of them to wear fun patterns and styles.

"Perfect," she said, holding them up.

"Not sure why you want to wear boots with pictures of barns and cows on them," Sam teased. "I hope we won't be getting into the cattle business."

She laughed. "No, but they didn't have any with goats or dogs!"

Sam smiled and urged Alice to open the rest of the presents that were piled up in front of her. He'd gone a bit overboard, but Taylor probably had, too.

Alice was just such a great kid and so easy to please.

"What is this one?" Alice picked up a small box and held it to her ear, shaking it gently.

"Something you've requested ..." Sam teased. "But something that comes with a lot of rules."

That hint did it. Alice shrieked and tore into the wrapping, quickly pulling out the latest Smartphone to hit the market.

Taylor wasn't too thrilled that, now, Alice might become one of the teenagers who kept their face glued to the screen, discarding books or interacting with their family, or nature. But Sam had assured her that he'd installed very serious parental parameters and would limit her screen time.

Thankfully they had a lot of years before they had to worry about Lennon interacting with the worldwide net of nutters. She was currently entertaining herself laying on her back under her new kick and play activity gym. It was crazy how long it had taken them to choose just the right one, before settling on the one that bragged different levels of learning with more than eighty-five songs, sounds, or phrases. Taylor secretly hoped that Lennon might be the first in her family to have some sort of musical ability.

Alice tore into another gift—this one the new book series

she'd asked for—and with one hand surfing through Diesel's hair for comfort, Taylor glanced at her phone.

Still no return message from Shane. Obviously, he was busy with the investigation, but she wanted to be in on it.

Word had spread fast, and now she knew that it was Jane and Willis, and their son Seth and his wife. Taylor knew Jane well from the post office when it was her turn to pick up the departmental mail. Jane was a good woman, and Taylor didn't know Will that well, but had only ever heard commendable things about him.

Their son, Seth, was in construction and had a solid reputation around town for being good at carpentry and fair on his prices. It was hard to get good tradesmen these days, to show up and do what they say they would for the price agreed upon, but Seth had never been hit with bad reviews on the community Facebook page, like most of the others.

To imagine four adults from their little community just gone in the blink of an eye ...

"Taylor, back to earth ..." Sam said.

She turned to him and smiled. "I'm here."

"No, not really. I know where your mind is, and you can't get involved right now. You and I both know that your health isn't up to par," he said, keeping his voice low. Alice had gone over to play with Lennon and was in the middle of pretending to eat her feet, creating a huge smile on the baby's face. She adored her big sister. Anytime they couldn't get her to stop crying, all they had to do was hand her to Alice. At only fourteen years old, Alice had more experience handling babies than most anyone Taylor knew.

"No, I was thinking about Lucy. Still haven't heard from her, and mom said she hasn't either." It was kind of true; her youngest sister *had* been on her mind that morning.

"Well, you know how she can be. I wouldn't worry too much."

"I'm just gonna walk over and see if she's at the cabin," Taylor said as she stood, reaching for the new cane. "Will you watch out for Lennon? She just nursed a while ago so she should be good until I get back."

"Of course. You don't have to ask me to watch out for my own kid, Taylor," Sam said, winking at her. "Hurry back though, because we'll miss you."

"I'll go with you," Alice said, jumping up from her place on the floor beside Lennon.

"Come on, then," Taylor said. Alice was just as protective of her as Sam, both of them thinking she couldn't venture around outside alone yet, in case she stumbled.

They got on their jackets and gloves, and Alice held the door. Diesel led the way out. The first blast of cold air felt refreshing. Taylor was so tired of being kept inside. Carefully, they made their way down the porch steps, holding on to the railing to keep from slipping.

Sam or someone had shoveled the walkways, so it wasn't too hard to make it to Lucy's cabin across the way. Actually, the whole farm looked nicely kept, the white snow glistening all around, paths marked with candy canes and red bows and lights hanging on the fencing.

"Ooh ... it's so pretty out here," Alice said, like she hadn't been in and out all day for the last week. Taylor is the one who hadn't had a chance to see everything, her mobility keeping her indoors too much.

Ellis and Sam had decorated their biggest tree that stood near the barn, and it stood tall and proud to be adorned with red and silver ornaments, sparkly white lights.

It truly was amazing to look around at everything they'd built over the last few years. Her once battled homestead with just a house and a lot of untamed land around it was now something they were all proud of, and grateful to have. Not only the cabins that Lucy, Jo, and Cecil lived in, but also their building for the boarding business, the barns for the rescue animals, and all the sheds and corrals put together with many hands, and even more hopes for the dream they had all built together.

Why couldn't she be happy with just all this? Why did she feel like no matter how much she did, it was never enough? For some reason, this wasn't enough to fill the deep well of her longing to do more, to protect and serve, and prove to everyone that she was much more than she'd began her life as.

Would she ever stop feeling like the poor, motherless kid who had to claw her way through her childhood? Her therapist said that feeling shame if she found herself relaxing was a trauma response.

"You're not more worthy of love as a result of working yourself to death, Taylor," she'd ended their session with.

If only it was that easy to just turn off that part of herself. To let go and enjoy this time with Lennon, and Alice. Embrace the slower pace and let herself take in every second of motherhood, before she went back to work. Cate had already offered to watch Lennon on the days that both Sam and Taylor worked the same hours. Thinking of leaving her baby made Taylor sad on one hand, but, on the other, it felt like the most responsible thing to do.

"Her curtains are closed," Alice said, jolting Taylor out of her deep thought. They'd arrived at Lucy's house and her car was in the driveway.

Hmm ... the curtains looked more than closed. The windows all appeared to have something over them, blacking out the view of the inside. She suddenly felt uneasy.

"Alice, I want you to go get Sam," she said.

She didn't want to put Alice into any danger.

"No way," Alice said, the lines on her forehead furrowing sharply. "I'm staying with you. What's wrong?"

Taylor tried to smile. "Probably nothing. I'm just being weird."

She climbed the porch stairs and went to the door, trying the handle. It was locked. She knocked, and they waited. No one came so Taylor knocked again, this time louder.

"Lucy, are you in there?" she shouted, banging her fist on the glass of the door.

They heard someone talking. Alice looked at her, wide-eyed.

Johnny was in there.

Taylor banged on the door again. "Lucy, I know you're in there. Open the door or I'll have Sam break it down!"

They heard Lucy yell at Johnny just before she jerked the door open.

"What do you want?"

She looked rough, her hair a matted mess and her face drawn and pale. Behind her, Johnny stood with an empty bag of Cheetos. He looked like he'd been crying.

Alice ran to him and knelt down, hugging him close before leading him to his bedroom. Taylor stepped in and waited for her eyes to adjust.

It was dark inside, but you could still see that the whole cabin looked a mess. The tiny kitchen was unkempt, stacks of dirty dishes on the counter among cereal boxes and other junk food containers. Blankets and pillows were strewn on the floor in front of the television. Rumpled and ripped wrapping paper scattered about. At least Johnny had opened his gifts.

It looked like they'd been camping out there for a while. Taylor was shocked to realize that the windows were covered with black trash bags tucked in behind the rods. And strangely, even the large decorative mirror over the sofa was covered with a bag, too.

She turned to Alice. "Get Johnny's coat and boots on and take him to our house. I need some time with Aunt Lucy, okay?"

Alice nodded solemnly. She was smart, and knew something was terribly wrong.

When Johnny was bundled up and they were out the door, Taylor noticed the mouse traps. There must've been fifty or more, all set and lined up against the back of the countertops, around the table and perimeters of the living room and kitchen walls, and all the way down the hallway.

Not a one of them had been activated. No mice. Just a lot of peanut butter blobs.

Taylor felt a wave of dizziness and she clutched the cane. She turned to Lucy again.

"Okay, this is what is going to happen. I'm going to stay calm, but you'd better start talking and tell me what the hell is going on."

# Chapter Five

ourage was the antidote for fear, and usually Taylor was leading the charge, but this time she sat unsure of what to do next. She was scared.

*No, she was terrified.*

After Alice had left with Johnny, things had only gotten more bizarre in Lucy's cabin.

Her sister was in trouble.

Not legally, but mentally.

They'd stopped talking a half hour before, when Lucy had broken down crying and claiming that someone was after her, and that they'd even sent planes overhead to find her.

Finally, Taylor found her voice again, stepping into her familiar role as the big sister and caretaker—the one who had always used logic to keep her sisters on the right path.

"Lucy, you know that we are right in the path that Lockheed Martin uses to test their new F-16s at least a few times a year. Don't be silly. No one is looking for you," she'd told her. "And what is with all the mouse traps?"

"I keep hearing them scurrying around in the walls, and cupboards."

"This is a log cabin. They can't get into the walls. And I haven't heard of a mouse being in any of our homes since we upped the number of barn cats on the property. Do you have proof that you have a vermin problem?"

In return, she'd gotten wide eyed swimming with fear. Then Taylor spotted a piece of paper on the table amongst the other clutter. Lucy had drawn a map of their property, outlining the fencing, little squares for the cabins. Bigger ones for the other buildings. It was complete with lines marking the trails they'd used as kids—one that went to the dock and lake, and others that circled back around the farm.

When she asked why the map, Lucy had shut down, refusing to say another thing.

Suddenly a commercial came on the television with the mayor of Atlanta saying she would take severe action against anyone who continued to commit crimes in their city, and Lucy started shaking.

"She's sending me a message," she'd whispered.

"Why would she be talking to you? You haven't lived around Atlanta in years."

Lucy continued staring at the television.

Taylor didn't know what to do or say. This kind of thing wasn't in her wheelhouse. She could deal with a criminal by using force or negotiation. Had Lucy lost her mind?

"I'm going to clean this place up," she'd said to buy herself time to think. "You can help, or you can rest."

Lucy parked herself in the very far corner of the couch, huddling under a big blanket.

"You missed our family Christmas dinner," Taylor said. "Everyone wondered where you were, but we thought you were tied up at the gallery. Last minute Christmas sales."

"I'm not eating anything I don't make myself."

Hmm ... that was interesting. Lucy was usually first in line at any of their family meals, as she wasn't fond of cooking for herself and Johnny.

"A friend I met in jail came to visit."

She wanted to keep talking, to pretend like things were normal until Lucy snapped out of it. "Her name is Quig. The one who threw the chair through the door to get them to take me to the hospital. It was good to see her, to see that she's trying to turn her life around. I think you would've liked her."

No reply.

Usually Lucy would be interested in stories like that. She was always rooting for the underdogs, having been one herself for so many years when she ran the streets. But she didn't react.

Maybe she just needed to rest.

It took a while but, when Taylor finished washing the last of the dishes and the dirty frying pans, she put everything away and wiped down the counters. She peeked into all the cabinets, under the sink, and even pulled out the warming drawer under the oven.

Not one mouse dropping to be found anywhere. No bugs, either.

She went to the living area and began picking up blankets, folding them and placing them neatly in Lucy's recliner, topping them with the bed pillows.

"What room do these go in?" she asked Lucy.

Her sister stared straight ahead, not blinking.

"Lucy, I'm talking to you. Stop ignoring me." She went to stand in front of her, and, awkwardly, she knelt down, looking into her eyes.

There was no movement.

"Why don't I help you into the shower, Lucy? We can wash your hair."

Nothing.

Taylor waved her hand in front of Lucy's face and there was

still no reaction. That's when a coil of fear snaked up her spine, crawling all the way to her brain. Her hands began to shake as she got her phone out of her pocket and texted her mom.

> Bring Ellis and come quick to Lucy's cabin.
> Something is wrong with her.

\* \* \*

Ellis held the stethoscope to Lucy's chest, listening intently. She hadn't spoken a word to them, and Taylor could see that Cate was trying not to look frantic.

When he looked up, his eyes were sad. "Let's step into another room."

Taylor led them to Lucy's bedroom. It was a disaster, but she'd never been big on making her bed, so it wasn't that unusual. She told them about the state of the cabin when she'd arrived, and the mouse traps, but no evidence of droppings in her search.

"The mice thing could be auditory hallucinations," Ellis said. He pushed a rumpled comforter back and sat on the bed, running his hand through his thick hair. "I've also seen it present in patients brought in high on methamphetamine, and a few other drugs."

Cate gasped, and Taylor put her head into her hands.

*Please, God. Not again.*

That she knew of, Lucy had never done meth, but she'd done a multitude of other drugs back in the day. And she'd gone missing for months at a time, so who knows what all she'd done during that time. Or was doing now.

Taylor looked up and she couldn't keep the anger out of her voice. "If she's doing drugs again, we have to protect Johnny."

"Now hold on, let's don't jump to any conclusions," Ellis

said. "There's a lot going on here, but, right this minute, she might be in akinetic catatonia. She's presenting with lack of movement and speech, but her vitals are fine."

Taylor felt sick at her stomach, and she lowered herself to the bed beside Ellis. Was her sister insane? All thoughts of being involved in the Colburn murder case had left her mind when she'd walked through Lucy's door earlier.

"Catatonic? What does that mean? What is it?" Cate asked.

"A neuropsychiatric condition. With it, a patient will freeze up, have trouble starting or finishing anything, and could stay in the same posture for hours."

"That could explain why the cabin is a disaster," Taylor said.

"How does that happen?" Cate asked.

He shrugged. "A lot of things can push someone into that state. Let me ask you, Taylor, has she ever been diagnosed with a mental illness?"

Taylor shook her head. "Not that I know of, but I've always suspected she might have something. When she was young, she was so rebellious. Impulsive, even to her detriment. She's never connected action with consequences. And she's always had super high highs, and very low lows."

"Sounds like a mood disorder, but I don't want to back alley diagnose her. I'm not a psychiatrist. She needs a full workup because there are some diseases that can cause this. Parkinson's, epilepsy, and we can't rule out a stroke, either, though my initial exam doesn't point to that. You also have MS and lupus as a possibility. Lastly, I had a patient just like this once, and eventually she was diagnosed with encephalitis."

"What do we need to do?" Taylor asked.

"The treatment is usually Benzodiazepines of some sort. Valium, Xanax—something like that. We'd have to get her to a hospital or a doctor to prescribe it. I can't prescribe any longer."

"We can keep Johnny with us, if you two can take her to be examined," Taylor said, looking at Ellis and Cate. "I hate it that he was here while she was going through whatever this is. I'd go but I really don't want to leave Lennon yet."

"Of course we'll take her," Cate said, going into the living room.

Taylor and Ellis followed. Lucy was still sitting in the same spot, motionless.

Cate knelt to her level, and picked her hands up in hers, warming them back and forth.

"Lucy, if you can hear me, we are going to take you to the hospital so you can get some help."

Like a jack-in-the-box, Lucy's eyes widened, and she popped up from the couch, wobbling on shaky legs as she took an aggressive stance.

They all recoiled, an involuntary response from the surprise.

"No! I'm not going anywhere! They're out there!" She pointed frantically—and with jerky, exaggerated movements—to the door, and her blackened windows. "Bring Johnny back to me. Now!"

Cate instantly enveloped her into her arms, hugging her close. Lucy was stiff and unwavering, but Cate continued holding her, whispering into her ear that she was okay. When Lucy's body finally relaxed, she slowly sat down again.

Taylor took the other side and put her arm around Lucy.

Ellis sat in the recliner, leaning forward with elbows on his knees.

"Lucy, listen to me," he started with a soft, soothing voice. "Johnny is with Sam and Alice, and he's safe and happy. You are having some sort of mental breakdown, and my professional opinion is that you need a full workup and possibly medication.

I know you're fearful, but I swear to you that these fears are lies that your brain is telling you, and everything is just fine."

Lucy was listening. And blinking.

That was a good sign. Taylor waited, not wanting to say anything that would make her sister freak out again.

When Lucy looked at Cate, her eyes questioning, Cate nodded.

"Ellis is telling you the truth, sweetheart. Everything is okay, but, please, let us help you."

"But the mice ... they won't stop making noise," Lucy said, putting a hand to one ear. "All day and all night."

"I've checked everywhere, Luce, and there is nothing to prove you have mice. I swear," Taylor said.

"But—" she looked so confused.

"Will you let me help you into the shower? We'll wash your hair and get you into some clean clothes before you go. Is that okay, Lucy?" Taylor asked. She had a memory from long ago pop into her brain. She'd helped Lucy shower before, when she'd snuck back into Della Ray's house covered in dirt and debris, smelling like pig manure and vomit, mixed with whiskey. She'd only been fourteen. Where she'd been was still a mystery.

"I want Mom to help me," Lucy said.

Cate nodded and helped her stand, then led her to the back bathroom. When they were gone from sight, Taylor met Ellis' eyes. They were just as sad as hers probably were. He hugged her and, when they parted, Taylor spoke, her words solemn and full of worry.

"So this is Christmas," she said, ending on a long sigh.

# Chapter Six

Taylor pressed her cheek to Lennon's soft hair, breathing in her baby scent while she wiggled sleepily in her arms. Johnny was curled up in the corner of the couch watching cartoons as he clutched his new stuffed dog they'd given him for Christmas. Adele was sitting nearby, enjoying spending time with Johnny while Lucy was "away on a jaunt," as she had been told.

Alice was sprawled on the rug in front of the TV, flipping through one of her art books, headphones over her ears, the cord leading into her new phone. Sam had debated getting her cordless ones, but ultimately decided those would be too easy to misplace.

Outside, as he worked on his client's car, his tools clinking once in a while from his shop, carrying over the chill evening air.

Ellis and Cate had been gone with Lucy for four agonizingly long hours. Taylor hadn't talked to Sam or Ellis about her plans yet, but she was already figuring out how to arrange Lennon's crib and dressing stand into the corner of Alice's room.

Just temporarily, so that they could move Lucy in until she recovered. Johnny sure wouldn't mind. He loved being there with them, especially Alice. He was also infatuated with Lennon, calling her 'their' baby. He wanted to be included with loving her.

When her phone vibrated on the armrest, Taylor's pulse spiked.

Cate's name lit up the screen.

"Hey," she whispered, inching further from Johnny, hoping not to disturb him.

"Taylor, it's me." Cate's voice was soft but edged with worry. "We're at the hospital. They've done some initial testing on Lucy."

Taylor's throat tightened. "And?"

"First of all, all the drug screens are clean. She's not taking anything."

Taylor released the breath she was holding and her shoulders dropped. "Oh, thank you, Jesus. Then what's going on with her?"

"They're leaning toward psychotic depression." Cate paused, letting it sink in. "She's going to get a full workup, though. MRI, CT scan ... bloodwork. Dr. Langston thinks they need to do a neurological assessment, too."

Taylor pressed her hand to her forehead, trying to force herself to focus. "Psychotic depression. That ... that means she's actually hearing and seeing things, right?"

"Yes," Cate replied. "She's still convinced people are watching her, tracking her. She's hearing voices at night, like whispers or sometimes faint music. She mentioned the mice again, too."

Taylor closed her eyes, rubbing her temples. "God, Mom, I don't even know what to do with this. All those things from when we were kids ... they're starting to make more sense now."

"Like what?" Cate's voice was gentle, urging her on.

"Lucy was always ... different," Taylor began, her voice low.

"And I do remember once she stayed in her room for a few days, not talking to anyone and barely eating or going to the bathroom. I thought she was just being dramatic. I should've seen it was something else and gotten help for her. Maybe it would've changed all the wrong choices she made later, as an adult."

Cate sighed. "Taylor, you couldn't have known. You were a kid yourself. You took care of your sisters the best that you could. You kept them safe and fed and helped them through school. Never take that away from yourself."

"Yeah, but there were other things. Like one time she locked herself in the bathroom for hours, convinced someone was spying on her through the mirror. Or when she'd disappear for days, only to show up again like nothing had happened. Dad and I thought it was just being 'rebellious,' but maybe ... maybe it was more."

Cate's silence hummed through the line before she responded, "I think it was. And that's why we're here now. We'll get to the bottom of it and find a way to help her."

Taylor wanted to cry. She still felt like her sister's mother. She held Lennon a little tighter, feeling the warmth of her small body steady her. This one would be protected and never have to worry.

She swallowed the lump in her throat before her next question. "How is she right now? Is she ... calm?"

Cate hesitated. "They gave her a sedative. She's ... stable, but she's not herself, Taylor. She's gone into a place that's hard to reach."

A thick, uneasy silence fell between them. Taylor wanted to cry, to scream, but all she could do was sit there, helpless, as her sister lay in a sterile hospital room miles away, probably terrified inside her mind.

"I think I need to come down there," she said, her voice small.

"No," Cate said softly. "You're still recovering yourself. I don't want this to make you slide back. Try to be calm and stay with the kids. I'll keep you updated, I promise. Let me be her mom, Taylor. You did it long enough and now you can rest."

Taylor took a shaky breath, nodding through sudden tears, even though Cate couldn't see her. "Thank you for being there."

"Of course." Cate's voice softened. "Listen, Taylor ... we'll get through this. We all will. Just hold onto that, okay?"

Taylor nodded again, feeling the weight of it all settling over her. As she ended the call, she glanced around her quiet living room, feeling the bittersweet ache of family and the harsh reality of their fragile world pressing in on her. Again.

# Chapter Seven

Shane glanced across the interrogation room where Missy Ann Colburn sat, her shoulders slumped, hands resting limply on the table. It was two days after Christmas, and the dark circles under her eyes told him everything he needed to know about the toll this nightmare had taken on her. He approached the table slowly, with the gentleness of a man who understood he was about to ask her to relive a horror she would give anything to forget.

He took a seat, folding his hands together. "Missy Ann," he started, his voice soft but firm, "I know this is hard, and I'm sorry to bring you in so soon after ... everything. But I need your help to make sense of what happened. Is that okay?"

Missy Ann nodded; her gaze fixed on a spot on the table as though she couldn't bear to look up. "I'll help however I can," she whispered.

Shane cleared his throat, choosing his words carefully. "We appreciate that. First, during the preliminary investigation, my deputy found your father's wallet and your mom's purse. They didn't look disturbed, and you said you didn't see anything missing from the home, so it doesn't appear to be a robbery."

"I agree. And I'm the one who set my parents up to pay their bills online, and I have their passwords. I checked their accounts this morning and there was nothing out of the ordinary."

"Okay, good job," Shane said, taking a note before looking up again. "Let's talk about your brother, Seth. I know he was a family man, good with the kids. But I also know work can sometimes bring out a different side. Did he have any enemies, anyone who might hold a grudge?"

Missy Ann shook her head slowly. "None that I can think of," she murmured, eyes still downcast. "Seth ... he was a good man, you know? Worked hard. Did everything for his family."

She hesitated, as if struggling with a memory, then looked up, her expression weary. "He's great at what he does—home renovations, custom work. People loved his skill, but ... sometimes you can't please everyone." She took a deep breath, the weight of her words settling in the air. "He's had a few disputes here and there. Mostly about money. Some went as far as small claims court, but nothing big. Nothing that I thought could ever ... lead to this."

"Do you think you could make a list for me?" Shane asked gently. "Anyone you know of who had issues with Seth? Just for us to look into, even if it seems minor."

Missy Ann nodded, biting her lip. "Yeah. I can try."

"Great. Now let's talk about your sister, Raya, and her boyfriend, Ronnie. What can you tell me about them that you think I should know?"

She shrugged. "I don't know. In my opinion, my parents have babied Raya too much, and it's why she hasn't found her lane yet."

"What do you mean by that?"

"Her career. Something she's passionate about. She's had a lot of jobs, and, when she got in trouble with her finances, they set that trailer up on the land and basically gave it to her. I told Mom that was just making her more dependent on them. I guess, because she's the baby, they feel that they have to make sure she's alright."

"Sounds like a bit of resentment there," Shane prodded.

She shook her head. "Nope. Not anymore. I'll admit, I wish I lived close and had as much free time as Raya so I could do more with Mom. They're always going shopping or something and sometimes I feel left out."

Shane wondered just how jealous Missy Ann was of Raya. And maybe even Erin. They were closer geographically to the Colburns, and probably did get a lot of one-on-one time that Missy Ann didn't get. Could it be a motive for her?

"When they go, does Erin join them?"

"Not usually. She's too busy with the kids."

"What about the boyfriend?"

"Ronnie? To be honest, I barely know him. He's come to some dinners and things at Mom and Dad's, but he doesn't talk much. He's a gamer, so he's always on his phone. But Raya is head over heels for him. They've been together about a year or so now, and that's a record for her, so I guess he's a decent guy."

"Did he get along with your parents? Maybe your dad wasn't happy about him moving in with your sister?"

"If he wasn't, he didn't say so. I think Mom was relieved, because it took some pressure off her to make sure Raya was doing okay and was happy. When Ronnie moved in, Mom had a lot more time to herself on the weekends. More time for the kids, too. Oh my God—I just can't believe she's gone," Missy Ann said, sobbing again as a new rush of tears sprinted from her eyes.

Shane pushed the box of tissues closer and gave her a soft smile, hoping it would ease some of the tension. "Thank you, Missy Ann. I know this isn't easy to think about." He paused, to let her collect herself, then leaned forward, speaking even more gently. "Can you tell me about your mom? I've heard from others that she was ... well, a really loved person."

Missy Ann's face softened, and a glimmer of warmth flickered in her gaze, though it was tinged with grief. "Everyone loved her," she said, her voice a little stronger. "She worked at the post office, you know? People looked forward to her mail routes; they'd come out just to chat with her. Sometimes they'd even leave her little notes or cookies, just because they knew she'd brighten their day."

"She sounds amazing," Shane said.

She smiled through a fresh wave of tears. "She truly was. She knew everyone by name, remembered their birthdays, their kids' names. She'd always say that people deserved to feel noticed, to feel like they mattered. And she made them feel that way, especially the ones who lived alone." Missy Ann let out a soft, broken laugh. "She and I talked every day, sometimes twice. I called her about everything. Mom was my sounding board and has talked me off the ledge more times than I can count. And the kids ... I can't stop thinking about them. They've lost so much. Not only Seth and Erin, but my parents were the best grandparents. Always there for them, every birthday, every school play, every little thing. My dad, he ... he'd take them fishing, build them little toys in his workshop. They were everything to him."

Missy Ann's composure finally shattered, and she covered her face with her hands, her shoulders shaking with quiet sobs. Shane sat still, he wanted to reach out, to offer some kind of comfort, but he knew that nothing he could say would take away the pain.

"I'll be right back," he said softly, standing and leaving the room. In the breakroom, he grabbed two sodas from the fridge.

As he turned, he almost ran into the sheriff, who eyed him

with a hardened expression. "How's it going in there?" Dawkins asked, his voice edged with frustration. "She got anything?"

Shane exhaled, rubbing the back of his neck. "Slow. She's grieving. No clear leads yet. But I'll keep pushing."

Dawkins' jaw clenched, and his face hardened. "Well, I called in the GBI. We can't afford to let this drag on, Shane. This kind of violence, this family ... we need answers, and we need them fast."

Shane stiffened, feeling a pang of irritation. "The GBI?" he echoed, trying to keep the edge out of his voice. "You think I can't handle this?"

"It's not that," Dawkins replied, though his eyes held a look that Shane couldn't quite read. "But we owe it to that family to bring in every resource. They deserve justice. Willis Colburn was my friend, and I won't let this case fall through the cracks just because we are a small county with even smaller resources."

Shane held back a retort, knowing this wasn't the time or place to argue. Instead, he gave a tight nod. "I'll find something, Sheriff. I won't let you down."

With that, he returned to the interrogation room, taking a steadying breath as he handed one of the sodas to Missy Ann. She accepted it with a grateful nod, wiping her eyes with the back of her hand as she tried to compose herself.

"Thank you," she murmured, opening the can with shaky hands.

Shane cleared his throat, gently steering the conversation in a new direction. "I wanted to ask about your dad," he said.

Missy Ann's eyes brightened, a trace of pride softening her grief. "He was the best dad someone could ask for. He never treated me any different than Seth and Raya."

"What do you mean?"

She reached up and wiped a tear away. "He's not my biological father, but he was always my dad. I was born before he met

Mom, and, when they got married, he adopted me. I don't remember a time that he wasn't my dad. He was a good, good man."

"I heard he was about to retire from Boeing?"

"Yes. Almost forty years as an engineer with them. It was the only place he'd ever worked. He'd talk about it like it was more than a job—a calling, almost. Worked on plans for planes, rockets, all kinds of projects. He was going to retire next spring. Along with Mom. They had so many plans."

Shane nodded. "Did he ever mention any issues with coworkers? Anyone there he didn't get along with?"

"No, he loved his job. He made really good friends there."

"Forty years is a long time, Missy Ann. Everything was perfect all those years? He never came home complaining of anything. That's sort of hard to believe. Sometimes the good guys get the shortest end of the stick in the workplace."

Missy Ann thought for a moment, then nodded slowly. "There was one incident, several years back. Dad worked with a man named Greg Chung for years. Well, Chung got arrested and was convicted for espionage, of all things. Turns out he was sending information back to China for something like three decades, if I remember right. He'd shared classified information about the space shuttle, and different military aircraft. It was a big deal. I think he got like twenty years in prison for it or something. But my dad ... he never liked him. Said he always seemed sneaky, even before the investigation. My dad wasn't the type to accuse people, and he's not one to discriminate against anyone. It was just that he had a bad feeling about that man."

Shane's mind raced, the information catching his attention. "Wait—do you know if your dad was the one who reported him? Was he the whistleblower?"

Missy Ann shook her head, a look of regret passing over her face. "I don't know. He never told us much about it, just that he was relieved when they caught him. My dad is—was—a very patriotic man. He was so angry that someone in his department was a traitor. Someone that close to him, and it had gone on so long before the guy got caught. Made him feel like a fool, and my dad didn't like no one making him out to be a fool."

The gravity of her words hung in the air, and Shane felt a chill creep over him. A spy, working closely with her father. It was a stretch, but could this have been revenge? Was Willis the one who'd found him out and reported him? And if he was, could someone from the People's Republic of China have sent someone to take out the family, years after the fact?

He was never one to buy into conspiracies, but this had to be checked out.

Shane forced himself to keep his tone calm, though his mind was racing. "Did they work closely together, you say?"

"Same department," Missy Ann replied, her voice a whisper now. "But my dad never trusted him. Even told us once that he thought the man was hiding something, long before anyone else suspected."

Shane leaned forward, his voice soft. "Missy Ann, I know this is a lot to ask, but if you remember anything—any conversations, something your dad might've mentioned about that—that could help us understand who might want to hurt your family, please let me know. It could make all the difference."

Missy Ann nodded, her face a mask of determination despite the tears shining in her eyes. "I'll try. I'll think on it, and I'll make that list for Seth, too."

Shane reached out, giving her a reassuring nod. "Thank you, Missy Ann. You're helping more than you know."

As he watched her leave, a strange, electric thrill coursed through him—a glimmer of a lead, however tenuous. He knew it was a long shot, but, if there was even a chance this espionage case connected to the murders, he would dig until he found out.

Because he wouldn't let the GBI, or anyone else, step in and solve this case for him. This family deserved justice, and he was determined to be the one to bring it to them.

Now, for the other sister.

* * *

Shane watched as Raya Colburn entered the room, moving cautiously, as though every step took all the strength she had. Where Missy Ann had sat with shoulders up, easy to approach with questioning, Raya seemed almost folded into herself, a quiet, reserved presence that contrasted sharply with her sister's more assertive demeanor. Her gaze fixed on the floor, and, unlike her sister's polished appearance, Raya, though bigger than Missy Ann, looked worn down, her hair pulled back in a messy bun and her clothes wrinkled, as if she'd just thrown them on without much thought.

He had to assume that Raya was closer, and this had hit her harder emotionally, considering she lived right there next to her parents.

She sat down—a bit timid, glancing around as if she wanted to be anywhere but here. Inwardly, he acknowledged that Raya wasn't as striking as Missy Ann. She had a more subdued appearance, plain but not unattractive if she put some work into it. He could see that she'd once had a quiet kind of beauty. He sensed she was the type who often faded into the background, a trait he'd learned could sometimes make people very observant. People often said the most around those they didn't feel compelled to notice. The people who stayed in the corner. With her sister and brother both being successful at business, it probably made her feel less than them. Intimidated, maybe.

"Raya," he greeted softly, settling into his chair. "Thank you for coming in. I know this is hard, and I'm really sorry for what you're going through."

She gave a small nod, barely looking at him. Her voice was soft, almost as if she was afraid to speak too loudly. "I'll help however I can," she murmured.

Shane folded his hands on the table, keeping his voice gentle. "I just want to understand more about your parents. Their lives, the people around them. Do you know of anyone who might have wanted to harm them?"

Raya's gaze finally lifted, her eyes wide with a kind of startled innocence. "No," she whispered. "I can't think of anyone. My parents ... they were good people. No enemies that I know of."

He nodded, leaning forward slightly. "Your sister mentioned a situation at your dad's work. Something about a former coworker involved in espionage. Do you know anything about that?"

She shook her head, looking uncertain. "I remember hearing something about it ... years ago. But I don't remember any details. Dad didn't like to talk about work stuff around us."

Shane made a mental note of her response, though he sensed she genuinely didn't know more. Maybe she was too young at the time. He decided to switch directions. "Your sister also mentioned an uncle," he said, watching her closely. "Your dad's brother that he wasn't on good terms with?"

Raya nodded suddenly, her brow furrowing slightly. "Oh, yeah. Uncle Clyde. She's right, he and my dad weren't on the best terms lately."

Shane arched an eyebrow. "Any idea why?"

She shifted in her seat, a faint hint of embarrassment crossing her face. "I think it was because Uncle Clyde wanted to bring his camper onto the property and live here. Dad told him no. Uncle Clyde pitched a fit and then left in a huff."

"Why wouldn't your dad allow it?"

A faint smile, laced with sadness, tugged at her lips. "Dad said if he let one wayward family member move in, they'd all start showing up with campers. He always had this saying, 'Once you open the door, it's hard to close it again.' I guess he thought it was a boundary he had to set."

"But they let you live on the property," Shane said.

"Yes, but that was just to give me a head start to save some money. Ronnie and I were planning to move soon. We want a condo, with a pool and a gym."

She didn't look like she was a fan of any gym.

"We had an apartment when Ronnie first came, but we didn't like it there."

"Oh, which ones? When did you live there?"

She gave him the name and the dates, and he scribbled it down.

"Come to think of it," Raya said, her finger to her chin, "Uncle Clyde told my Dad that he didn't deserve to have all that land and should be sharing it."

"Was the land in the family before your dad?"

"No. He and Mom bought it. My uncle has no stake in it, so I don't know what he's talking about. He can be off the wall at times, though."

Shane considered this, filing it away. Family conflicts, however small, had a way of festering. "I see. Well, about your uncle, I might need to talk to him, just to cover all our bases."

Raya nodded, though her face remained impassive. "He was sad to hear about Dad. They weren't speaking, but ... Uncle Clyde's still family."

Shane let a moment of silence linger, then steered the conversation toward a different topic. "Raya, can you tell me a little about your brother, Seth? What was your relationship like with him?"

Her expression softened, a nostalgic warmth flickering in her eyes. "We were super close, all through school. He was my best friend for a long time. But after he married Erin and had the kids ... well, things changed. We drifted."

Shane gave her a sympathetic look. "Does that make you sad?"

She shrugged, a hint of defensiveness in her tone. "Not really. I have Ronnie now, and he's all I need."

Shane paused, curious about her relationship with this man who'd come into her life from across the country. "How did you meet Ronnie?"

Her cheeks flushed slightly, and she looked down at her hands. "It was online. A gaming site. We started talking in the chat, then moved to private messages. Over time ... we fell in love."

He nodded, noting the faint pride in her voice despite her reserved demeanor. "So, he moved here from California?"

"Yeah. We didn't want to keep doing long-distance, and I didn't want to leave Georgia. My family's here," she replied, glancing away. "He left everything to be with me."

"And I understand the two of you were planning to get married?" Shane prompted.

Raya's face fell, and she let out a sigh. "Yeah. We were actually going to elope. We chose Christmas Eve, thinking it would be special ... now, I wish we hadn't picked that day." Her voice cracked, and she swallowed hard, as if trying to keep her composure. "After everything that happened ... we still aren't married."

Shane sensed a lingering regret, as though the failed wedding plan was both a point of sadness and guilt for her. "I'm sorry things didn't work out as planned."

She nodded, forcing a small, sad smile. "Me, too."

He let a moment of silence pass before clearing his throat and asking, "One last thing, Raya. Is there anything else you can think of—anything at all—that might be relevant? People, incidents, anything out of the ordinary?"

She shook her head, looking down again. "No ... I wish I could help more, but I don't know anything that would make sense of this. I'm just ... so lost."

Shane gave her a reassuring nod, leaning back in his chair. "You've helped a lot, Raya. Thank you for coming in. I'll walk you out."

As he watched her leave, he felt a growing sense of urgency. Raya was reserved, but there were threads there—family tensions, a fiancé from out of state, an estranged uncle—that all warranted deeper investigation. And then there was the espionage thread, however tenuous. Shane had a feeling the answers weren't as far away as they seemed.

But he knew he needed to move fast before the GBI took the case over.

# Chapter Eight

Shane stepped into the sterile, chilled confines of the medical examiner's office, the air heavy with the unmistakable blend of antiseptic and something darker, a faint lingering of death that clung to the walls. The fluorescent lights were harsh, illuminating the rows of steel tables, their surfaces gleaming coldly under the clinical light.

Dr. Fenton, looked up as Shane entered, setting aside his notes with a grim expression. His face was ashen, worn down from the weight of what he'd seen in recent days.

"Shane, good to see you. Sorry about the circumstances," Dr. Fenton greeted with a nod, gesturing to a set of files on the table. "You ready for this?"

Shane took a deep breath, steadying himself. He didn't look around the room. Didn't want to. The actual scene from the Colburn property was still in his head, vivid enough. He didn't need to add one more. "Yeah, but I don't need to see the victims. Just give me the details. Let's start with Willis Colburn."

Dr. Fenton sighed, flipping open the first file. "Mr. Colburn had blood on his face, dirt on his shirt, and his clothes were bunched up in odd places. There were bruises and scratches on his back—signs he'd been dragged."

That was when they'd dragged him through his own living room, outside, off the porch and around back, then dropped him like a bag of trash on the deck of the shed.

Shane's jaw clenched. "How ... how quick was his death? Did he suffer?"

"It was quick, I'd say." Dr. Fenton pointed to an image, showing the entry wound at Willis's temple. "The bullet went straight through his skull. Death was likely instantaneous."

Shane closed his eyes briefly, imagining the scene, the horror of it. "Any sign he tried to fight back?"

"None," Fenton replied. "No defensive wounds. Toxicology came back clean, too—no drugs or alcohol in his system. It was a single, direct shot. It's likely he didn't see it coming."

Shane nodded, feeling a bitter mixture of relief and dread. At least Willis hadn't suffered long. But what about the others?

"What about Jane?" he asked, his voice a little rougher.

Dr. Fenton opened another file, his gaze somber. "Mrs. Colburn was found lying on her back in the middle of the shed. Before they moved her, I saw blood on her thigh, but there was no wound there. It looks like the blood from her head wound dripped down onto her leg because of the way her body arranged itself when it was thrown in there."

Shane swallowed hard, remembering Jane lying there, lifeless, in a pool of her own blood as he'd seen her days ago. "And the gunshot wounds?"

"Two bullet wounds, though I believe three or four shots were fired. The first shot, close range, hit her in the forehead." Fenton tapped the photo showing the stippling marks. "She was likely looking up at her killer when it happened. That shot would have incapacitated her, and she wouldn't have been able to breathe but she'd still be lucid."

Shane felt his stomach twist. He didn't want to imagine Jane in that moment, staring up at the gun, terrified and knowing what was coming. "And the second shot?"

Fenton's expression was grim. "It went from her neck down to her shoulder and lodged near her armpit. The hollow point bullet fragmented, tearing through her body. I can't tell for sure which bullet came first, but she likely felt both."

Shane gritted his teeth, anger simmering beneath the surface.

Fenton continued. "There were abrasions on her arm, her hand, and her hip," he confirmed, flipping through the images. "Not defensive wounds, but they're consistent with the body being dragged, too."

Shane's fists clenched. He could almost see it—the killer, heartless, dragging Jane's lifeless form. "And Seth?"

Fenton moved to the next file, and his face tightened. "Seth had blood on his face, his stomach, his thighs. He had a head wound, a neck wound, and an abdominal wound. The head wound was downward, through the chin, into his chest."

"Standing over him?" Shane asked, voice barely above a whisper.

"Most likely," Fenton replied. "And the abdominal wound? That one went straight through his stomach and out his back. It's seared, blackened at the edges. That shot was fired close up, but it wasn't the fatal one."

Shane's voice was tight. "Why?"

"No bleeding around the site. It was postmortem. They shot him again even after he was gone," Fenton said, his voice low.

The thought was sickening. Shane's throat tightened, bile rising. "This ... this wasn't just murder. This was annihilation."

Fenton nodded solemnly, and then opened the last file. "Now, Erin Colburn. Hers was ... complicated. Six bullet tracks. It's almost impossible to say the order of the shots, but it all happened fast. One bullet entered her forehead, close range, like Mrs. Colburn."

Shane's breath caught. "So she saw the gun, too."

"Yes. And she had multiple shots to her chest and abdomen. Her body showed signs of movement while bleeding. The killer or killers ... they weren't in a hurry. They took their time even as she fought to live."

Shane felt a cold fury building. "This was a slaughter," he muttered, his voice shaking.

Fenton nodded, his face weary. "Yes, I'm afraid so. Whoever did this, they wanted them to suffer. They wanted to make a statement."

Shane turned away, feeling the weight of the case like a vice around his heart. He clenched his fists, forcing himself to keep it together. Thank you, Dr. Fenton," he said, rage simmering inside as he turned and left the room.

# Chapter Nine

Shane sat in his truck in front of the diner. He had ten more minutes before his meeting. He should probably call Mira. He'd gone to her house last night but fallen asleep before she even got out of the bathroom and into the bed. She probably wanted an explanation.

Instead he opened his laptop and then his inbox to find two new emails since he'd last checked. He wondered if Sam knew that Taylor was helping on the case. She couldn't be there in person, and Shane had told her he could handle it without her, but she wouldn't take no for an answer.

He read through it quickly.

Shane, here's what I found on Erin (Hurst) Colburn. Age 32, she graduated high school fifteen years ago in Jasper. She was an A student and a member of their drill team. After graduation, she attended the Spruill Institute of Arts in Dunwoody, Georgia, and did a few years in community college in Jasper. She and Seth got married a year after she graduated college. She worked as an assistant bakery manager at Pastry Perfection. Seth, also 32, graduated high school the same year, but from Hart's High. He lettered in football, track and wrestling. He got a business degree from Mercer and went into construction. He's had his own company for about fifteen years and was a member of the Carpenters Union. I'll follow up with some details on Raya and Ronnie probably in a few hours. It's time for Lennon's lunch. -Taylor

Her background search pretty much matched up to what he'd learned from Seth's sisters. He replied to her and asked her to find out what she could on Willis's brother, Uncle Clyde, then he opened the second email that had come two hours later.

Raya. She's 29. Graduated from Hart High School. I pulled her yearbook records and saw she was on the cross-country team and part of the art club. I also reached out to one of her former teachers. They described her as a sweet and artistic girl, though not exactly a social butterfly. She wasn't part of the "in-crowd," but she had her own group of friends. Didn't attend college. Currently, Raya works at a video game store. Raya and her brother were listed in public business records as co-owners of an auto painting company about four years ago, but I couldn't find a website for it, so it might've closed. Raya sometimes helps out as a postal carrier for her mom. She met her boyfriend, Ronnie, about a year ago on an online dating site. He works at a Target in a mall in Jasper. Before moving to the mobile home on her parents' property, Raya and Ronnie lived in an apartment complex. I spoke with the apartment office manager, who remembered them, but nothing out of the ordinary.

As for Ronnie, I haven't uncovered a ton yet, but I did manage to get in touch with his brother, George. He described Ronnie as a "spiritual kind of guy," whatever that means. There are three siblings total, and his brother had some nice things to say about him. Apparently, Ronnie used to stick up for George in school because he had a speech impediment and was bullied for it. I probed a bit more and found out that Ronnie has a blood disorder and suffers from chronic nosebleeds, which kept him out of sports in school. Instead, he's more into books and video games. George said the last time he heard from Ronnie, his brother was really excited about marrying Raya and talked about wanting to have kids soon. Let me know if you need me to follow up on anything specific. -Taylor

Shane had already searched the trailer where Raya and Ronnie lived, after they'd given permission. Other than being a total rat hole, he'd found nothing. Their truck had been searched by Deputy Gonzalez while Shane was taking photos of the two, and—wait ... there was one thing. He shot another email off to Taylor.

Raya and Ronnie had trouble with the engine running hot in their truck, as well as a flat tire the day the Colburns were found. They decided to cancel the trip to Vegas they were on the road for and turned back after they used Frank's Flat Tire Fixit, outside of Asheville. Confirm, please.

He looked at his watch. Eleven sharp. He got out and adjusted his collar as he entered, unsure what kind of man to expect.

Ed Sorenson was a retired Boeing engineer. A friend of a friend had made the connection, and Shane knew he was lucky to get even this lead. No one in Boeing's higher ranks had agreed to talk. But Ed Sorenson had agreed to meet, and that was as close as he could get.

The smell of fresh coffee and bacon drifted through the air as he scanned the booths. A gray-haired man sat near the window, his worn navy jacket draped over the back of his chair. He looked up as Shane approached, and his eyes crinkled with recognition.

"Detective Weaver?" he asked, standing to shake Shane's hand.

"That's me. Thanks for coming out, Mr. Sorenson. I appreciate you taking the time."

"Just call me Ed. And no problem. Anything to help Willis's family." Ed's voice grew gruff, and he cleared his throat. "Still can't believe they're just gone, like that." He snapped his fingers in the air and then let his hand drop to his lap.

They sat, and a waitress came over to take their orders. Shane opted for black coffee and a banana bran muffin, while Ed asked for his "usual," which earned him a wink from the waitress. He looked like a regular here, comfortable in the small-town diner ambiance. They made small talk until their coffee arrived, but Shane could see Ed's expression was weighted with grief.

When the waitress walked away, Shane decided to ease into the questioning. "You knew Willis well, then?"

Ed nodded, swirling his cup with a spoon, creating slender milky clouds on the surface of his coffee. "Willis and I were in the same department for twenty-five years. We weren't just colleagues; we were friends. Hell, he was like the brother I never had. Jane—his wife—she used to pack extra food for me sometimes. She knew I didn't have anyone to cook at home. Willis would show up with a lunch big enough to feed a family, and he'd just grin and say, 'Jane thought you could use a hot meal, Ed.' She made the best meatloaf I ever had in my life. Lord, I'm gonna miss that woman." His voice cracked slightly, and he took a sip of coffee, looking away for a moment.

Shane smiled sadly. "Sounds like they were special people."

"They were." Ed shook his head slowly. "Never met anyone with a work ethic like Willis's. He was old-school. Didn't put up with any nonsense and always had everyone's back. People like him don't come around often."

There was a pause, and Shane let it sit before moving forward. "I wanted to ask you about Greg Chung. I know it's been years since that happened, but, from what I've heard, he didn't exactly make a lot of friends at Boeing."

Ed let out a bitter chuckle. "That's putting it mildly. Chung was ... a strange guy. Creepy, if I'm being honest. Kept to himself, never joined the group for lunch or a beer after work. We all tried to include him, figured maybe he just felt like an outsider, you know? There weren't a lot of Asian guys in our department back then, and we wanted to make him feel welcome." Ed paused, shaking his head. "But he was always standoffish, didn't want anything to do with us. We'd catch him staring at people in this ... weird way, like he was studying them. Gave us all the creeps."

"How did he manage to get classified documents out of Boeing? I mean, the place has some of the tightest security out there," Shane pressed.

Ed scratched his head, his brows knitting together as he thought. "Look, Boeing had its protocols, but no system's perfect. Chung was smart, knew the ins and outs. He must have used a combination of memory, concealed storage, and just plain brazen moves. There were times he'd stay late, saying he was catching up on work. We thought he was dedicated, but now ... now I know he was just using that time to sneak around."

The waitress came and brought Shane's coffee and muffin. A plate of bacon, fried eggs, and a plump biscuit for Ed. A side of apple butter.

Shane leaned forward, his voice low. "Ed, I need you to be

completely straight with me here. This could be the difference between finding who killed Willis's family and this case going cold. Was Willis the whistleblower? Did he report Chung?"

Ed's face darkened, his gaze hardening as he met Shane's eyes. "No. Willis wasn't the whistleblower." His voice held a fierce pride. "But if he or I had known what Chung was up to, we would've dragged him straight to corporate ourselves. That bastard betrayed all of us, not just the company, but his team. Our country, too. Right under our noses. You think that sits well with any of us? Hell, it tore Willis up that we hadn't figured it out. Made him feel ... responsible, like we'd all failed somehow. But we had nothing to do with that investigation."

Shane watched Ed closely, catching the subtle tremor in the older man's hands as he took another sip of coffee. The betrayal clearly still stung, even years later.

"Did Willis ever talk about his family to you? His brother, specifically," Shane asked, shifting gears.

"Clyde?" Ed snorted, a look of distaste crossing his face. He picked up his biscuit and sopped up some of the runny yolk of his eggs. "Yeah, I know Clyde. Even went fishing with him and Willis once. Big mistake."

"Why's that?" He was liking old Ed. It was always great to get to interview a talker in the middle of an investigation. Someone you didn't have to pull information out of, and you could sit back and let it flow.

Ed swallowed his bite of eggs and leaned back, crossing his arms as a look of irritation flickered in his eyes. "Clyde's a leech. A piss-poor loser, too. He spent half the day sulking because I reeled in the biggest fish. Claimed it was 'his spot' and that I'd stolen it from him." Ed rolled his eyes. "Man acted like a big baby. Couldn't handle anyone else's success, especially not Willis's. Always felt his brother should bail him out of whatever mess he'd gotten himself into."

75

Shane filed this away, sensing the family tension simmering beneath Ed's words. "Willis ever mention why he didn't want Clyde around?"

"Sure. Willis said if he let one wayward family member settle on his property, the rest would start showing up with their hands out. And knowing Clyde, he'd find a way to drag everyone down with him. He didn't want that for Jane, or for the kids and grandkids when they visited. His place was meant to be a sanctuary, not a charity." Ed's jaw clenched, and he looked out the window, a faraway look in his eyes. "Willis did his best to help Clyde over the years, but there comes a time when you gotta cut people loose, you know? He told Clyde he'd help him find a place, even tried setting him up with work, but Clyde always managed to screw it up."

"When's the last time you remember Willis having Clyde out at the property?"

Ed shrugged. "Since I retired, I don't get to talk to Willis that often, so I couldn't tell you. But if you're thinking ol' Clyde has something to do with this, I really doubt it. He's not only a leech, but also a coward. He was bigger than Willis in stature, but he'll never be the man his brother is. I mean, was."

Shane took a deep breath, weighing the pieces of information he'd gathered. "I appreciate your honesty, Ed. I know this can't be easy."

Ed nodded, his expression softening. He finished off his biscuit and eggs with one last bite and chewed on a piece of bacon. "I just hope you catch the bastard who did this. Willis didn't deserve it. Neither did Jane. Or Seth and Erin. It's a damn shame, is what it is." He pushed his coffee cup aside, getting to his feet. "Thanks for hearing me out, Detective. I'm glad someone's taking this seriously."

"Do you know where Clyde lives?"

"Sure do. He's renting out the back of an old dive bar out

past Poole's Mill Park in Ball Ground. It can't be more than one or two rooms, and the building is about falling down. They closed the bar at least ten years ago, and they should've bull-dozed the whole rotten place. It's not in any shape to be living inside and I guess that's why he was so eager to move to Willis's place. Thank God Willis didn't let him in."

Shane rose as well, reaching out to shake Ed's hand. "Thanks, Ed. You've helped more than you know."

Ed held Shane's gaze for a long moment, then nodded. "You find out who did this, you give them hell for me. For Willis. My brother from another mother, as we liked to say."

With that, Ed turned and walked out of the diner, his shoulders a little slumped, his hands shoved deep in his pockets. Shane took out his wallet, paid for their meals, and headed for the door, his mind buzzing with questions.

* * *

Shane's stomach let out an annoyed growl as he eased the car onto an old county road, surrounded by dense, darkening woods on either side. The afternoon was slipping away, and he hadn't eaten since the quick cup of coffee and a muffin that morning. Meeting with Ed had run longer than expected, and now he was paying for it. He'd just have to tough it out until he got back to Hart's Ridge; he had no idea where to find a good meal in Ball Ground.

The small town was eighty miles of winding, weathered asphalt from the diner. The narrow roads snaked through small clusters of houses, meadows, and thick woods. He used the time to catch up on calls, including his mom and Mira. His signal went in and out a few times, making conversation difficult, but at least he'd checked in. Sadly, the more time he and Mira spent apart, the less he missed her.

They might not last as long as he and Lucy had, and he'd thought that was a short one. He should've known not to try to date any of Taylor's sisters. It was just weird.

He passed a herd of deer grazing on the edge of a field, their heads lifting in unison as his car approached. A possum darted across the road, narrowly escaping his front tire, and Shane muttered a low curse, steadying his grip on the wheel.

Up ahead, Deputy Kuno's cruiser was parked on the shoulder of the road, the glow of his hazard lights visible through the trees.

Shane pulled up behind it and climbed out of his car.

"Cutting it close, Weaver," Kuno called, stepping out of his car and stretching. His German Shepherd, Valor, leapt out after him, moving with practiced precision to heel at his side. Lately the dog was with him all the time, and the sheriff hadn't said a word about it. "I've been here for fifteen minutes, and, you know, there's a highway that would've got us here faster."

"Figured I'd let you get the scenic view," Shane replied dryly. Once again, he wished it was Taylor being his back up. She never complained.

Kuno smirked, gesturing toward the long driveway that snaked into the woods. "Not much out here but trees and critters. You sure about this lead?"

Shane nodded. "Ed's intel might be sketchy, but it's all we've got. Clyde Colburn's a wild card. If there's dirt there, we need to dig it up."

"Fair enough. Valor's ready to go if we need him," Kuno added, giving the dog an affectionate scratch behind the ears.

From what Shane had seen of the dog, he wouldn't harm a fly.

Somewhere close, a dog started howling, then broke into a frantic bark. Valor's hair stood up but, with a few soft words from Kuno, he settled.

They only walked five or so minutes before the dive bar Ed had described came into view, its rusted metal sign hanging crookedly from a chain above the door. The building looked like it hadn't been maintained in decades—weathered siding, cracked windows, and a sagging roof. Around the side, a battered van sat on flat tires, its back window patched with duct tape and a garbage bag. A scrappy dog was chained to a dilapidated wooden doghouse, a stainless-steel bowl over-turned just out of his reach. No water to be seen. He'd worn the ground down to dirt five or so feet all around the doghouse. Inside wasn't even a stick of straw to keep him warm.

"Classy," Kuno muttered.

"Fits the profile," Shane said as they approached the door.

"Someone needs to come rescue that fellow. Might have to sneak out and cut the chain myself."

The dog continued barking, leveling into a more frantic tone.

Valor sniffed the air but remained alert and steady at Kuno's side as Shane knocked on the warped wood of the back door.

No answer.

Shane knocked again, louder this time. Kuno circled to the front entrance, Valor padding silently beside him. "Place is dead quiet," Kuno said when they regrouped.

"Maybe he's not home," Shane started, but the sound of muffled cursing cut him off.

"Who's making all that racket?" a gruff voice called from inside.

Shane knocked again, his patience thinning. "Detective Weaver with Hart's Ridge Sheriff's Department. Open up, Clyde."

After another shuffle of footsteps, the door creaked open to reveal Clyde Colburn. His greasy hair stuck out at odd angles, and his rumpled clothes looked like they hadn't seen a wash in weeks. He reeked of stale beer and something sour.

He bellowed at the dog to shut up, then turned back to them. "What do you want?" he grumbled, squinting against the fading daylight.

"I'm here about your brother, Willis," Shane said, flashing his badge.

Clyde's expression darkened. "Yeah, yeah, come on in. And in my opinion, dogs shouldn't be allowed indoors, but I'll make an exception for a police dog. Don't let it piss all over my floor."

Shane almost laughed. You could barely see the floor from all the junk piled around it, and what could be seen was far from clean.

"Don't worry," Kuno said as he stepped inside with Valor. "He's better behaved than most people."

The inside of the place wasn't any better than the outside. A grimy mattress leaned against one wall, surrounded by crushed beer cans and crumpled takeout containers. A sagging armchair faced an ancient TV, and the air was thick with the smell of mildew and stale smoke. What was once possibly a nice mahogany cocktail bar ran along one side of the room, scratched, beaten, and piled high with items and boxes.

One battered bar stool graced the front.

"Make yourself comfortable," Clyde said sarcastically, flopping into the armchair. Other than the precarious-looking barstool, there weren't any other seating options. "What's this about, then? You gonna solve Willis's murder?"

"That's the plan," Shane said, crossing his arms as he assessed the man in front of him. "I understand you and your brother didn't get along."

Clyde snorted. "That's no secret. Willis thought he was better than me. Always rubbing his nice house and land in my face while I have to scrape by."

"You think that justifies what happened to him?" Kuno asked, his tone sharp. Valor let out a low, rumbling growl, as if echoing the sentiment.

Clyde shifted uncomfortably. "I didn't say that. And before you ask, I wouldn't hurt my own brother, no matter how much of a pain in the ass he was."

"Where were you the day of the murders?" Shane asked, his gaze steady.

"Workin'," Clyde snapped. "Morning shift at the scrap yard. The boss had me inspecting a truckload of scrap metal some rednecks from Calhoun brought in. Talk to him if you don't believe me."

"We will," Kuno said, jotting the information down.

"What about Jane?" Shane pressed. "I've heard you were fond of her."

Clyde's face softened. "Jane was good people. Always kind to me, even when Willis wasn't. Sends me a plate every Thanksgiving. He couldn't stand it that she treated me right. She didn't deserve what happened."

"And Seth and Erin?"

"They were good kids," Clyde said, his voice quieter now. "Seth was just like his mama—kind, hardworking. I didn't know Erin but I'm pretty sure she didn't deserve it either."

Shane studied Clyde for a moment, noting the shift in his demeanor. "When's the last time you were at Willis's house?"

"Years ago," Clyde said quickly.

"What about when you asked to park your camper there?"

"I stayed outside the gate," Clyde replied, his tone defensive. "Asshole wouldn't let me come in. Blood don't mean nothing these days. I sold the damn thing after that."

Shane exchanged a glance with Kuno, who nodded slightly.

"We're going to need a DNA sample," Shane said.

"You already got it," Clyde shot back. "From that fraud

charge Willis pinned on me years ago. The one where he accused me of stealing his social security number and racking up credit card debt in his name? It was a setup, and I caught a felony for it."

"Did you serve time?" Kuno asked.

"Just probation," Clyde muttered. "Willis told the judge he didn't want me locked up. Made me do community service at the animal shelter. He thought it was punishment, but the joke was on him. That's where I got my dog, and I got lucky—he's a hell of a security guard."

Shane felt sorry for the dog. Living his life on a chain wasn't lucky.

"Well, Clyde, if you think of anything else—anything at all —you call us," he said, turning to leave.

As they walked back to the cars, Shane glanced over at Kuno. "What's your read?"

"He's holding something back," Kuno said, giving Valor a pat. "Valor picked up on it, too. Clyde's nervous, but not enough to scream guilty. Could just be the guilt of a crappy brother. Sensing some infatuation with Jane, too. What's that commandment, don't covet your brother's wife?"

"Something like that," Shane said, glancing back at the dilapidated house. "But I've got a feeling there's more to his story. I'll be anxious to see what forensics find in the DNA."

# Chapter Ten

Taylor embraced the impending feeling of chaos that she knew would soon settle around her, as it painted her willpower with a new sense of purpose. She set a flashlight on the nightstand, along with a glass of water and a granola bar. Sam had moved a queen-sized bed out of Anna's guest room, carried it over in his truck, and set it up in Lennon's nursery, making plenty of room for Johnny to sleep with his mom. They'd taken the crib and dressing table out, putting it in Alice's room. There wasn't much they could do about the pale-yellow walls and nursery theme, but she was doing the best she could for the situation. Alice had easily agreed to let Lennon stay in her room for a while without any fuss at all, but Taylor hoped it wouldn't be long.

A teenager needed her own room. And a baby needed a very quiet environment.

Alice would be quiet when Lennon was sleeping, but she couldn't tip toe around completely. There were bound to be some commotion and sleepless nights before everyone settled in. Especially tonight, because it was New Year's Eve and, no doubt, someone close would be setting off fireworks, creating havoc with all their animals who would be terrified and thinking the world was coming to an end.

Cecil, Ellis, and Sam had worked hard all morning to make sure all the fencing was tight, and no one would try to bolt through any escape patches during their fright.

"What's this for?" Lucy asked, pointing at the unopened box in the corner of the room.

"Oh, Sam's dad got it for the baby, but we aren't going to use it. Sam read up and found some bad reviews. It's like a little nest that's supposed to keep the baby feeling snug in the crib, like they're in the womb. The elevated cloth sides are the problem, as Lennon could snuggle into it and suffocate."

"Oh. Yikes. Why don't you take it back? Get a refund?"

"Probably will eventually. It's just not easy for me to get out and do stuff like that yet."

Lucy plopped down on the bed. "Exactly. And that's why I shouldn't be here, adding more stress to you. I swear, I'll be fine at my house."

Cate had tried to talk Lucy into coming to their house, but Lucy felt that, if they were going to insist she couldn't go to her own cabin, that Johnny would be happier where he could interact with Alice and the baby.

Taylor was tired, and she'd been sneaking back and forth to her room and computer, trying to at least do research for Shane. Something to feel a part of what was going on. To help find who had wiped out the Colburns. Sam didn't know it yet, and she felt bad for keeping it from him, but she didn't want to hear any flak.

It was going to be harder to sneak around with Lucy there, but she'd manage.

"Let's not argue about this again, please." She sat beside her sister and pulled a pillow onto her lap to snuggle. Lucy's official diagnosis was *depression with catatonic features*, but Taylor wondered if it was really more than that. They'd only held her for five days, and how could you really know anything in that short amount of time? "How are you feeling? Do you want to talk about what it was like there?"

"I'm feeling fine, and it was boring as hell. They treat you like you're crazy there," Lucy said. "After the ER evaluation, they took me to a small building on the same hospital campus. I don't remember much of that day, but I woke up the next morning to a nurse drawing my blood and I nearly punched her in the nose. They shouldn't sneak up and do shit like that when you're sleeping."

Taylor chuckled. That was her youngest sister, always ready to fight.

"So did they do any kind of counseling?"

Lucy nodded. "Yep. Like three times a day. And we weren't allowed to sleep between the meetings. There was no access to computers. We had a day room with a couch and chairs, but it was always something ridiculous on the TV. Believe it or not, I spent a lot of time reading. Cate brought me a few books. One was called *The Secret Life of Sunflowers* and, man, was it good. I learned a lot about Van Gogh and his struggle to be recognized, and the support he got from his brother and sister-in-law. He spent a year in an asylum before he died. It sure made me feel better about my circumstances."

Taylor laughed. "Well, I think that—back then—people were sent to asylums for just about anything, but I'm glad you got some time to rest and read. Maybe you really needed it, Lucy. You've really been working hard building your art consulting business. Too hard."

"Yeah. And to be honest, I'm tired of trying to go through life trying to fix or improve myself for the sake of everyone else. From now on, I'm just going to be me, whatever it is."

That didn't sound good. They all needed to work to improve

themselves—or be a better version of themselves, Lucy just as much as everyone else, but now wasn't the time to go deep. Taylor changed the subject.

"Could you go outside at the clinic?"

"Yeah, we had a small yard to exercise but it was surrounded by a tall fence, like we're in prison. The medication window was insulting, too. You go for your meds, and they hand it to you in a tiny paper cup, then you have to take it and show them your mouth so they can confirm you swallowed it. They wake you at six in the morning and hand over your hygiene bag. When you finish brushing your teeth, washing up and putting on the deodorant, you have to hand it back in, so, yeah ... they treat you like you are crazy. And let me tell you, there were a lot of people in there who weren't crazy. They were smart and funny. Some of them just brought in for a day or two after getting picked up high or drunk and brought to the ER."

"I know one way they can avoid ending up there," Taylor said.

"Yeah, yeah, I know. The food was decent, though. We got one cup of coffee a day, and it wasn't great, but the meals were okay. To be honest, it kind of felt good for the strict routine, and having a time without having to make any choices or decisions. Just did what they told me to do, but I missed Johnny terribly. I don't want to be separated from him like that ever again."

Taylor hoped it never happened again, too. "Do you think the counseling helped?"

Lucy shrugged. "Not really. Some of our group meetings were just us sitting around requesting songs and the leader would play it on her phone for us. Those weren't bad. I hated the meetings with the social worker. One meeting she had everyone close their eyes and go back to one of their worst experiences in their mind. She had some of them bawling their eyes out. I don't think that was helpful at all."

"Did you go back to one?"

"No," Lucy shook her head. "I've got plenty of really traumatic experiences I ran into on the streets, around Atlanta and in New York. Even with my son's sperm donor. But God knows I don't want to relive any of them."

"Don't you think that talking about it might help?"

"Sure don't. Don't want to talk about it to her, or you, or to anyone else. What I've learned over the years on the rare occasions I've been dumb enough to open up to someone is that people have a lot to say about lives they've never lived."

Taylor wished so hard that she could help Lucy. She was just so tough, but she needed to find a way to open up to someone or she was never going to heal from the things that had happened in her past.

Alice peeked in the door, then came in, Johnny on her shoulders.

"Look, Mama," he said, smiling from ear-to-ear.

"Oh my goodness, you're so tall!" Lucy replied.

Johnny cackled out, his laughter ringing through the house.

If there was one thing that Taylor knew for sure, it was that Lucy loved her kid more than anything. But did she love him enough to get serious about getting her mental health on track?

# Chapter Eleven

Shane stood in Sheriff Dawkins' office at eight o'clock sharp for their meeting, the air between them tense. Dawkins leaned back in his chair, fingers steepled, his eyes sharp. "So," he said, voice taut with impatience, "tell me you have something concrete."

Shane's jaw tightened. He knew what case Dawkins was talking about. As far as the department was concerned, there was only one case right now. Everything else was on the back burner. He dived in with what he had.

"CSI is clearing out of the Colburn's property as we speak. I asked them to rush the DNA, but you know how that goes. I guess GBI will help it along some, though."

"That's all you've got?"

"No." Shane pulled a sheaf of papers from the folder under his arm and put them on the desk in front of the sheriff, before taking a seat. "Here's the final report from the medical examiner."

Dawkins flipped through them and Shane could see him trying to keep his expression bland, but he cringed when he got to the first photos. When he finished, he looked up and a tic could be seen working quickly in his jaw.

"What else?" he asked through clenched teeth.

"Phone records are coming soon. Jane's eldest daughter knew her Facebook password and I looked at it briefly but will go through it more thoroughly today. Willis doesn't do social media. We don't have the passwords for anything on Seth and Erin yet, but I'll look through their posts."

*That was the next task he was handing over to Taylor.*

"Kuno and I talked to Willis's brother, Clyde Colburn. He's got an alibi at the scrap yard, though ..." He hesitated, knowing Dawkins wouldn't like the answer. "They don't have a time clock or badge system. I had to go by the boss's word."

Dawkins scoffed, slapping his hand on the desk. "So we're just taking his word for it? Damn it, Shane. We need something solid here! If we don't start narrowing down suspects, this whole thing's gonna slip through our fingers."

"I'm aware," Shane replied, struggling to keep his own irritation in check. "But for now, Clyde's in the clear. I checked it out. His boss confirmed and the camera at the gate has him pulling in and parking. We already have his DNA in the system and, if it shows up in that house, we'll put him at the top of our list. I also talked to one of Willis's close co-workers who was around during the whole Chinese espionage case. He says he and Willis had no idea there was spying going on and weren't a part of the discovery. Willis definitely wasn't the whistle blower."

Before Dawkins could respond, the door creaked open, and Dottie from dispatch appeared, her face white as a sheet. She clutched a file in her hands, her fingers trembling slightly.

"What is it, Dottie?" Dawkins asked, his brow furrowing at her expression.

"Sheriff, there was ..." she trailed off.

"Spit it out. What's going on?" Dawkins said.

She let out a huge sigh, her eyes wide with fright. "There was a 911 call made from the Colburn house on Christmas Eve," she said, her voice barely above a whisper. "But ... no one said anything on the line. It sounded like maybe it was at a party, and it disconnected."

Sheriff jumped to his feet, his face flushed with anger.

"And you're telling me that no one checked it out?"

She took a step back. "Deputy Penner was dispatched to check it out but reported back that the gate to the property was locked. He decided not to go further, and we both thought it was a false call." She swallowed, glancing at Shane, then back at Dawkins.

Dawkins shot up from his chair, his expression hardening. "Are you serious here? Penner went to the scene and didn't investigate further?"

Dottie nodded, her eyes dropping to the floor. "Yes, sir."

Shane felt a pit form in his stomach. That call could have been a lifeline—a chance to intervene and maybe even save one of them. And it was squandered.

Dawkins gritted his teeth, and his voice dropped to a dangerous low. "Thank you, Dottie. Get Penner in here. Now."

Dottie hurried out, and the office fell into silence, thick and charged. Shane could feel the tension radiating off the sheriff, the frustration simmering beneath the surface. Moments later, Deputy Penner shuffled in, his face red, shoulders hunched.

Dawkins didn't waste time. "Why the hell didn't you tell us about the 911 call?"

Penner's face fell, his gaze dropping to the floor. "I ... I was ashamed, sir," he mumbled, voice barely audible. "I didn't think it was relevant at the time. The gate was locked, there was a no trespassing sign on it, and I had no reason to enter without probable cause ..."

Dawkins clenched his fists, barely restraining himself. "Ashamed? Ashamed that you left a potential crime scene unchecked? You might have had the chance to stop this tragedy, and you're telling me you kept it quiet out of shame? This is going to make us look like a pack of damn fools to the GBI team."

Shane couldn't take it anymore. He stepped forward, his voice calm but firm. "Sheriff, if I may—it's standard protocol. If nothing was said on the call, the gate was locked, and there was nothing else suspicious to go on, crossing that gate would've been illegal entry. Penner was following the rules. It's not his fault."

Dawkins turned to him, eyes blazing, before finally exhaling in frustration. "Fine. Get out, Penner," he barked. The deputy glanced at Shane, murmuring a quiet thanks before he hurried out, his face flushed with embarrassment.

Once they were alone, Dawkins took a deep breath, running a hand over his face. "You got anything else for me?"

Shane's mind raced back over the notes he'd taken that morning. The reports from Taylor, too, though he couldn't bring her name into it. Dawkins would have his ass if he knew she was working the case, even if only a tiny bit, remotely.

"Preliminary backgrounds on Colburn's youngest daughter and her fiancé are good. The flat tire story checked out, and a call with Ronnie McGill's brother was met with nothing but good stuff about his big brother protecting him when they were kids and now being some kind of spiritual gentle giant. I had Penner running reports from county probation officers. All their criminals are checked in and accounted for, nothing stirring up interest there. I subpoenaed the phone records for all four, to see who they were communicating with that morning."

"Like I told you, GBI has one of their top guys on this now.

He's taking over the conference room and wants us to work together." He looked at Shane, raising an eyebrow. "You in?"

Shane's jaw tightened. He wasn't ready to hand it off or share credit. "I've got Deputy Kuno for support and we're doing just fine. I'll move my stuff out of there now."

Dawkins sighed, shaking his head. "Fine, but don't get in the way of the GBI. They've got a top-of-the-line forensics team, and much more investigative technology sources than we do. This isn't about who gets credit; it's about finding justice." He turned, grabbing his hat and slamming the door behind him as he left.

Shane bit the inside of his cheek, feeling the bitter taste of resentment settle in. They'd been just fine using their own technology and outsourcing forensics. This was personal now. He'd solve this one his way—whether Dawkins or the GBI liked it or not.

# Chapter Twelve

The porch swing creaked softly as Taylor eased into it. She pulled her sweater tighter against the cool January air, her gaze shifting to Sam. He sat beside her, baby Lennon nestled against his shoulder, her tiny fingers curling into the fabric of his shirt. Taylor had layered blankets over her, even though Sam was enough of a heater, himself.

She noticed that the shutters needed painting and a board in the porch bucked, begging for a nail to tap it down. Cate and her sisters all lived in new houses, and, except for Lucy's home's disarray, their homes were neat and flawlessly arranged.

Taylor didn't mind at all. There was no envy in any part of her bones because her house had seen them through a lot of memories, hardship, and accomplishments. The fact that it was still standing, and was now the dwelling for a whole lot of love, made it perfectly imperfect for her and her little family.

Diesel lay stretched out at their feet, his ears twitching toward the distant yips of coyotes.

"Sure you don't want me to put her down inside?" Taylor asked softly.

Sam shook his head, his eyes on Lennon's peaceful face. "Not yet," he murmured. "Feels like I haven't seen her all day."

Taylor smiled faintly, leaning her head against his shoulder for a brief moment. She was so tired. "You're a good dad, you know."

Before Sam could respond, the sound of footsteps on the gravel path drew their attention. Diesel looked up, but didn't react, so they knew it was someone he knew.

Cate and Ellis appeared, walking side by side from their property across the way, bundled against the chill. Cate carried a thermos, and Ellis balanced a couple of mugs in his hands. Taylor waved them over, shifting to make room on the porch.

"Thought we'd bring you some hot chocolate," Cate said as she stepped up. "Figured you two were out here enjoying the quiet."

"Yes," Taylor said with a grateful smile. "But company's always welcome."

"As long as you're keeping my little tadpole nice and toasty under there," Cate said. She reached over and pulled Lennon's blanket up an inch or so, tucking it around her neck.

"She's so warm she's making me hot," Sam said, chuckling.

"This fresh, crisp air is good for her," Ellis said, "but in small doses."

He handed Sam a mug, then poured another for Taylor as Cate settled into one of the porch chairs. He took the chair beside her, stretching his legs out in front of him. "How's she doing overall?" Ellis asked, nodding toward the baby.

"Perfect," Sam said, a soft smile spreading across his face. "Couldn't ask for a better baby."

Diesel huffed softly, his ears flicking at the sound of more coyotes. Cate leaned over and gave him a reassuring pat before turning her attention to Taylor. "How's Lucy?" she asked gently.

Taylor hesitated, glancing at Sam. "It's ... been rough. I peeked into her room earlier when I went to call her for dinner, and it's a disaster. Dirty dishes discarded here and there, clothes all over the floor. Looks like a cyclone hit."

Cate frowned, worry creasing her features. "That sounds like more than her usual mess."

"Oh, it is," Taylor said. "It's like she's regressed back to being a teenager."

"I try not to say anything, but my pet peeve is that she's leaving wet towels on the bathroom floor," Sam added, his tone edged with frustration. "And toothpaste smeared in the sink. It's like she's not even trying. I guess the only positive thing I can add is that she mostly stays to her room, so the mess isn't spreading too far. She brought her TV over and set it up, and she turns the volume up to drown out the sound of mice scurrying around. Mice that we don't have."

Taylor had forgotten about that. She felt sick to her stomach now.

"What about Johnny? Is she taking care of him?" Cate asked.

"Not really. We've all teamed up and Alice is a big help," Taylor said. "He'll do anything she says. Even eat his vegetables, just to please her. We've gotten him on a good schedule and routine, and I've seen he thrives because of it."

"Kids always need structure and routine," Ellis said, nodding his approval. "Their daily lives are in the hands of adults, and they usually don't have any say. At least if they know what to expect, it helps them keep balanced when the chaotic times come around. His life has been turned upside down and of course he's gravitating toward what is solid. But let me ask you this." He leaned forward, resting his elbows on his knees. "Do you think that Lucy is taking her medication?"

"I really don't know," Taylor admitted. "She's been avoiding work and ignoring calls. Faire called to check on her and said that Lucy isn't returning any of her messages. They usually talk daily. Oh, and Lucy keeps insisting she smells something burning. For the first few nights, she had us checking every corner of the house, searching for the source. I think she's still paranoid, even though you've explained to her so many times what's going on in her brain is making her suspicious of things."

Ellis nodded thoughtfully. "It's not uncommon for people in her state to resist medication or fall into old patterns. The paranoia, the manic behavior—it could all be part of her cycle."

Taylor sighed, her shoulders slumping. "I just don't know how to help her. She won't open up to me, and everything I say feels like it makes her pull back even more."

Cate reached over and squeezed her daughter's hand. "You're doing everything you can, sweetheart. But Lucy has to want the help. She has to meet you halfway."

Sam shifted on the swing, his arm tightening around Taylor. "We'll figure it out," he said firmly. "But Taylor's already stretched thin. Between Lennon and everything else, she doesn't have time to be cleaning up after Lucy, too. If this keeps up, Lucy is going to have to go. She'll have to go to your house or move back into her own cabin."

"No, she's not ready to be alone," Taylor said quickly. "Especially with Johnny. And he's so happy here."

"I'll talk to her," Cate said quietly. "Maybe she'll listen to me. I can remind her about her routines, and we'll see if we can ease her back into some kind of normalcy."

"That's a good idea," Ellis said. "But we'll have to keep an eye on her. If she's not taking her medication or if her behavior gets worse, we might need to step in more seriously again."

Taylor nodded, though the thought of pushing Lucy further worried her. "She's just so closed off. I don't know how to get through to her."

Cate's expression softened. "We'll all be here for her. For you, too."

The conversation lulled, the group falling into a companionable silence. Taylor leaned into Sam, letting his warmth and steady presence calm her nerves. Lennon stirred briefly against his shoulder before settling again, and Diesel sighed deeply at their feet.

"It's going to take time," Ellis said eventually, his voice low and reassuring. "But we'll get her through this. One step at a time."

Taylor had to admit, it was different to have others to help her try to keep Lucy on the right path. For so many years, she'd felt solely responsible if her sister lived or died. Ellis said *we'll get her through it.* Now as Taylor looked around at the people she loved—her husband, her mom, and even Ellis—she let herself believe it and the weight shifted a tiny bit, letting her breathe.

# Chapter Thirteen

Murder investigations tended to move slower than molasses in the deepest of winter, but Shane had gotten lucky. It had only taken a few days to get back the phone records of Jane and Willis Colburn. He was still waiting on those for Seth and Erin, but hoped to get them by day's end, too. Seated in his office, Shane flipped through the pages of call logs and text transcripts from Jane's phone.

Most of it was unremarkable: messages from Seth about their travel plans, notes from Erin asking Jane to pick up the grandkids after school a few afternoons earlier in the month.

But then, a particular thread caught his attention—exchanges between Jane and a number labeled from an account named Cotton. He pecked the phone number into his computer, and it came up for Cotton Timmons, a man he was well familiar with, a neighbor of the Colburn's, be it with thirty or so acres between them. Shane saw Timmons all the time at Mabel's, walking in with a big belly and an attitude to match. Probably a shitty tipper, too.

He skimmed through quickly, eyebrows raising at the tone of the conversation.

. . .

December 23, 10:15 a.m.

> Timmons: "When are you finally going to deal
> with that damn dog? It's on my property
> AGAIN this morning."

December 23, 10:17 a.m.

> Jane: "It's not on your property. It's on our
> shared line. Calm down."

December 23, 10:19 a.m.

> Timmons: "Shared line, my ass. I'm not putting
> up with this anymore. Next time I see it, I'm
> calling animal control—or worse."

December 23, 10:24 a.m.

> Jane: "You wouldn't dare. Leave my dog alone,
> Cotton. We've been neighbors for years. Why
> are you acting like this now?"

December 23, 11:45 a.m.

> Timmons: "Because I'm sick of you and your
> damn husband thinking you own this
> mountain. Keep your mutt and your junk to
> yourself. Consider this your last warning."

. . .

Shane leaned back in his chair, frowning. The hostility was blatant. He flipped a few more pages, finding one final exchange late that evening.

December 23, 7:30 p.m.

> Jane: "We're not doing this tonight, Cotton. You've been drinking, haven't you? Stay off my property. If you come near us or my dog, I'll call the sheriff myself."

December 23, 7:32 p.m.

> Timmons: "Try it. See how that works out for you."

Shane's lips pressed into a tight line. He didn't like the implications. Had Jane showed Willis the conversation and things escalated? He flipped through Willis's messages quickly, but didn't see anything to or from Timmons.

That didn't mean anything.

Grabbing the folder, he pushed back from his desk and headed for Dawkins' office. "Sheriff, I'm going to pay a visit to Cotton Timmons," he said as he leaned through the doorway.

Dawkins glanced up from his paperwork, raising an eyebrow. "Timmons? What for? What's he up to now?"

Shane held up the phone records. "Maybe just running his mouth but there were some heated texts between him and Jane

Colburn the day before the murders. Threats. He's already got a reputation for being a hard-ass and I want to see how angry he actually was that day."

Dawkins narrowed his eyes. "You think he's good for it?"

"I think it's worth looking into," Shane replied. "At the very least, I'll see what kind of alibi he's got."

The Timmons' property was as unwelcoming as Shane expected. Rusted fencing surrounded the yard, and an old pickup sat in the driveway, its tires half-buried in the mud. A rooster and a few chickens roamed around, free-ranging and pecking in the sparse grass. A mangy looking dog barked furiously from behind a chain-link enclosure.

Shane knocked on the door, stepping back to give whoever answered plenty of space. After a moment, the door swung open, revealing Cotton Timmons. He looked to be in his late fifties, with a scruffy white head of hair and eyes that were equal parts bloodshot and suspicious.

"What do you want?" Timmons barked.

"Cotton Timmons?" Shane asked, though he already knew the answer. "I'm Shane Weaver with the sheriff's office. I'd like to ask you a few questions about your neighbors, the Colburns."

Timmons scowled. "They're dead. What about them?"

Shane crossed his arms, keeping his voice steady even as fury burned through him. "Yeah, I know they're dead. I'm leading the investigation and I'm looking into some recent incidents involving your neighbors. I've heard that you've had some issues with their dog. Care to elaborate on that?"

Cotton leaned against the doorframe, his gaze narrowing. "Yeah, I have issues. That mutt keeps wandering into my yard, scaring my chickens into a tizzy. I warned them plenty of times to keep it out."

Shane raised an eyebrow. "You sent Jane some threatening messages the day before the murders. Care to explain that?"

Cotton's jaw clenched. "I was pissed off. Can you blame me? That damn dog ate the leftovers I threw out to my hens. I didn't do nothing illegal, though."

"And where were you the whole day of December 24?"

He bristled. "Home. By myself. Watching TV. You can ask my dog."

"December 25$^{th}$?"

"Same spot. Same dog."

Shane didn't smile. "All alone on Christmas, huh? No one else can vouch for you?"

"Nope. Now, you done? Or are you gonna try pinning this on me just because I didn't like those people?"

"Will you take a DNA test?"

"Do you have a warrant?" Cotton asked, his face reddening.

Shane stared at him for a moment, letting the silence stretch. "We'll be in touch," he said finally, stepping back toward his truck.

As he drove away, he couldn't shake the feeling that Timmons was hiding something. Whether or not it had to do with the murders was another question entirely.

# Chapter Fourteen

S hane was in his office and felt a wave of frustration when he checked his email and saw that Taylor hadn't gotten back yet about the Colburn's social media. Moving on, he was halfway through organizing his notes from the Cotton Timmons interview when the phone on his desk buzzed. He picked it up to find Missy Ann, the Colburns' eldest daughter on the line.

"I just wanted to call and get an update," she said. "Do you have anything yet? We're having visitation down at the funeral home tomorrow and I know people are going to be asking."

She sounded sad and defeated.

"I understand, Missy Ann, but you just tell them the investigation is ongoing, and you can't talk about anything like that."

"But do you? Have anything, I mean?"

He sighed. "We're working on it. You focus on the rest of your family and getting through this tragedy."

"I'm trying but I don't think we're going to be able to do that until we have answers, Detective Weaver. Is there anything I can do to help? Please, anything at all."

He paused. "For the most part, no, but I did want to ask you about one of your parents' neighbors. Cotton Timmons. Does that ring a bell?"

"Yes, I know who you're talking about. They weren't friends —Cotton and my parents. He's a jerk."

"I've gathered that," Shane said. "It appears that he was angry about a dog crossing into his property, possibly killing his chickens."

She scoffed over the phone. "He said that, but Biscuit wouldn't hurt a flea. He's the gentlest dog in the world. Also, my parents had chickens for a while, and he would lay right in the middle of them and never react whatsoever. Daddy told Timmons he wanted proof that Biscuit did anything wrong or was even on his property and, the next thing you know, Mama found a bag of dog crap in the mailbox. Wasn't tied up in a bag either and she stuck her hand right in it getting the mail."

"And you think Timmons put it there?" Shane asked, taking a note.

"Well, what do you think? I mean—it's pretty obvious. Daddy called him and told him they were going to put a camera up and, if they caught him anywhere near our mailbox or on our property, he was going to have him arrested for trespassing."

"Sounds like it got ugly."

"It did, but that happened last year. That I know of, it all simmered down."

"Oh, okay," Shane said. People could hold grudges for a long time, and he wasn't going to tell her about the recent text messages from Timmons to her mom. He didn't need her flying off the handle and accusing Timmons of the crime before the investigation put together more. They at least needed his DNA before he lawyered up.

"Will you be at the funeral home tonight?" she asked, her voice soft again.

"I'm not sure. I'll try."

She paused. "I have just heard that, in crimes like this, sometimes the killer will come around the services. I thought you might want to look around and see who is there."

"That's not always true but, if I can make it, I will. I would definitely like to see the sign-in log if you put one out. Also, Missy Ann, as we are collecting DNA, I wanted to ask you if you can think of anyone other than family who was in your parents' home recently? Any neighbors? Timmons? Cleaners, repairmen—anyone that you know of so that we can begin an elimination process."

"No repairmen or cleaners. My parents did everything on their own and Daddy could fix anything. He did the kitchen remodel himself, along with help from Seth, and sometimes Ronnie. Oh, Mama's Bible study group met there sometimes but it's been a long time since it was her turn. I know because she always invites me, though I never go. I probably should. I should've been spending every minute I could with her. If I could go back ..." she trailed off.

"Okay, Missy Ann. I think that's all I have for you right now. I'll call you if anything else comes up," Shane said. He didn't want to be talking to her if she started crying.

They said their goodbyes and he'd just hung up the phone when it rang again.

"Hello."

"Shane, the sheriff wants you in the conference room," Dottie's familiar, curt tone came through the line.

"What's going on?" Shane asked, though he had an idea.

"Those two GBIs are here. Both of 'em look like they've never set foot in the woods a day in their lives. Dawkins wants you to bring him—and them—up to speed."

Shane exhaled sharply, his irritation already mounting. "On my way."

He grabbed the Colburn case notebook and headed for the

conference room. The low murmur of voices spilled into the hallway before he even reached the door.

Inside, Sheriff Dawkins sat at the head of the table, looking like he hadn't slept in days. Flanking him were two sharply dressed strangers. The woman had an air of quiet authority, her dark suit crisp and professional. Her hair was pulled back, her posture rigid, her eyes sharp as they scanned the room. The man beside her had a slightly more casual air, his jacket slung over one chair and his tie loosened, though the intensity in his gaze betrayed his laid-back exterior.

The massive board against the wall had grown since Shane last saw it. The photos of Jane, Willis, Seth, and Erin Colburn stared back at him, along with images of the snowy property, bloody footprints, and evidence bags. A web of red string connected time-stamped photos and notes. It was the kind of thing the GBI loved—big and theatrical, designed to intimidate and impress.

He had his own version on the wall in his office, but much less busy and dramatic. He didn't need to see their faces staring at him every day from the board; they were already imprinted in his mind. And in his notebook.

"Weaver," Dawkins said when Shane stepped in. "Let me introduce you. This is Special Agent Maeve Hanson and Agent Jared Tuffin from the Georgia Bureau of Investigation."

Shane nodded to each of them, shaking their hands in turn. "Detective Shane Weaver," he said.

"Detective Weaver," Hanson said, her voice as no-nonsense as her appearance. "As you know, we've been brought in to assist. Sheriff Dawkins says you've been leading the legwork on this case."

"That's right," Shane replied, taking a seat at the table.

"Good," Tuffin said, leaning forward on his elbows. "We're two weeks in without a prime suspect, so I think it's best that we all work on the same team from here on out. Sorry to put you on the spot like this, but I'd like to hear a full update, start to finish from your notes so far. Let's see where we're at and figure out where to go from here."

Dawkins gestured for Shane to begin.

Shane felt his blood pressure rising and throbbing in his body, but he took a deep breath, setting the Colburn notebook on the table and flipping it open. "You already know the basics —Jane and Willis Colburn, along with their son and daughter-in-law, Seth and Erin Colburn—were all found dead on the morning of December 25th at the family cabin. Jane and Willis were located outside, in and in front of an outbuilding, while Seth and Erin were found inside, one in the living room and the other in the kitchen."

Hanson's sharp eyes flicked to the board and their photos as Shane spoke. "Cause of death?"

They already knew this, but Shane complied.

"Multiple gunshot wounds for all four. Preliminary forensics suggests the same weapon was used for all the victims, based on the bullets recovered. None of the four slain Colburns owned a weapon matching the shell casings found, so we're working on the assumption it belonged to the killer."

"And no weapon recovered?" Tuffin asked.

"Not yet," Shane said. "The property's pretty vast, and I still have deputies and forensics—as you know—combing through it. Tomorrow I'll be out checking more local pawn shops and gun stores for any recent purchases that match the weapons used."

"What about signs of forced entry?" Hanson asked.

"None," Shane replied. "The house doors were locked, no broken windows, and nothing inside looked disturbed beyond the violence itself. It's possible the killer was someone they knew or trusted enough to let inside."

Hanson nodded thoughtfully, jotting a quick note on a pad in front of her.

Shane continued. "We've got the phone records for Jane and Willis. They didn't tell us much, except for a heated text exchange between Jane and a neighbor, Cotton Timmons, the day before the murders. Timmons has a reputation around town for being difficult, and the texts included some pretty explicit threats about their dog." He paused to pull out the relevant pages and slid them across the table toward Hanson and Tuffin. He didn't include the notes about the call with Missy Ann or the suspicion that Timmons put excrement in the Colburns' mailbox.

Hanson skimmed them quickly, her lips pressing into a thin line.

"This is new to us. Has Timmons been interviewed?" Tuffin asked.

"Yes," Shane said. "He admitted to sending the texts but denied having anything to do with the murders. Says he was home all day on the 24th and 25th with no alibi except his dog."

"And you believe him?" Hanson asked, her expression neutral.

Shane shrugged. "Hard to say. He's got a temper, but nothing solid yet ties him to the murders, and he has a somewhat firm alibi. I'm waiting on Judge Crawford to sign a warrant for his DNA so we can see if we can match anything at the scene."

"Good," she said. "I'll make sure that's expedited. If he's lying, I want to know."

"I've already asked it to be rushed," Shane said, his tone even. "The judge is aware of the circumstances."

*What did they think? That he was an idiot?*

"I want a stab at him," Tuffin said. "Schedule him again, for tomorrow."

"I can give you his number," Shane said. He wasn't anyone's secretary. Tuffin could do his own damn scheduling.

"What about the other neighbors?" Tuffin asked.

"I've talked to a couple of them," Shane replied. "Most didn't see or hear anything unusual, but they did mention knowing about the longstanding tension between the Colburns and Cotton Timmons over the dog situation."

"And the family angle?" Hanson pressed.

Shane hesitated and decided not to mention Clyde Colburn. He wasn't done with him yet and didn't want Tuffin stomping on it. "Still working on interviews but, so far, nothing of note. The bank records for the senior Colburns are on the way, but the eldest daughter has looked through and already said nothing is out of the norm. The Vegas story from their youngest daughter who lives on the property with her fiancé so far checks out. All way down to a statement from the dispatch of the service they called to change their flat tire. I've done some background intel on both of them, Raya and Ronnie, and it's all average small town citizen stuff. They both work retail, and my deputy has verified their employment."

"And Erin Colburn's mother? Wasn't she on scene first?" Hanson asked.

"Yes, she was. Nancy Hurst. She was first on scene and discovered the first two bodies, unfortunately. We've interviewed her a few times now, but she hasn't offered much insight as to any motives floating around out there. She claims her daughter and son-in-law are squeaky clean."

Tuffin nodded, satisfied. "Alright. So tell me, what's your read on this so far, Deputy Weaver?"

Shane frowned, leaning back in his chair. "My gut says this wasn't random. The killer knew the family and likely had a specific motive. It could possibly be tied to the dispute with

Timmons, or something financial with someone else. But until we get more evidence, it's hard to say."

"Agreed," Tuffin said. "But let's not rule out the possibility of a hired job. If the Colburns were involved in anything shady, that could explain the level of precision here. I want every public record on anything they've bought or sold in the last two decades."

Dawkins grunted. "Shady or not, they weren't exactly the type to have enemies. This is a small town, and everyone knew the Colburns as a quiet family."

"You can put one of the deputies on gathering the public records," Shane said. "I'm working on my own list of priorities first."

Hanson stood, crossing to the board and studying it in silence for a moment. "Alright, here's the plan. Weaver, you stay on the neighbors and family. See who else you can dig up. Get those financials and phone records processed ASAP. The sheriff and I will handle the warrant on Timmons, and we'll serve it. Tuffin, you dive into the Colburns' history today and see if there's anything in their past worth killing for. Anything Weaver may have missed."

Shane nodded, though his jaw tightened. He hated the way Hanson took control like this was her case. But talk was talk, and Shane had every intention investigating where and what he wanted to, without waiting on Hanson's orders or permission.

"We'll regroup tomorrow morning," Hanson said. "By then, I want updates on all fronts."

Shane left the room feeling both determined and frustrated. Dawkins was right on his tail and cornered him at the end of the hall.

"Check that attitude, Weaver," he warned. "And you'd better not be holding anything back from the GBI or you might just find yourself pulled off and out there investigating something else, like whose dog shit on the town square this week."

"Noted." Shane kept walking. It was ironic that Dawkins mentioned the dog shit, but he still wasn't giving that detail up yet. He also wasn't going to check his attitude. This was his town, his case, and his people. If GBI thought they could swoop in and solve it without him, they had another thing coming.

# Chapter Fifteen

Taylor leaned back against the headboard; her laptop balanced on her thighs as she clicked through Jane Colburn's private messages. It was tedious work, scrolling past conversations that could only be described as achingly mundane. There were messages to her adult children—reminders about a doctor's appointment, a forwarded recipe for her chicken casserole. A cheerful back-and-forth with her friend, Pam, about their book club, and a polite inquiry to a Marketplace seller about a vintage settee Jane had been eyeing. Nothing of interest. Nothing suspicious. Just snippets of a life that seemed ordinary, even boring.

She sighed, her fingers rubbing her temples. Shane had warned her it might be a dead end, but Taylor wasn't used to finding nothing. She wanted a lead—something, anything to help solve this mystery. Instead, it was just another reminder that crimes like these didn't come with a flashing neon arrow pointing to those responsible for the carnage.

A nap for herself would be blissful, but she didn't have time.

It had been a busy morning. She'd reorganized Lennon's clothes, boxing up the newborn items she'd long outgrown, and bringing more of her current clothes into Alice's bedroom for easier access. After that, she'd sat down and organized all of Sam's business receipts that he'd thrown haphazardly into a box.

Thankfully Anna took care of the family boarding business accounts, but Sam was always running to town to buy parts and supplies, then tossing his receipts around the house for Taylor to keep up with. Next, she'd have to check his Amazon account to pull a list of items purchased for business. Once she had everything together, she would enter it into their accounting ledger to prep for tax time.

Alice wanted to go shopping, to spend the gift cards she'd gotten for Christmas, and Taylor had put her off, but she needed to make time to do that, too.

She'd washed all the clothes that were piled around the house, including Johnny's and some of Lucy's. When she thought she couldn't move another muscle, it was time to put Lennon down for her nap, along with Johnny, and then get on with trying to do some research for Shane for the Colburn case. She was thankful that Willis didn't seem to have wanted any part of social media, making her job a lot easier.

She opened a message from Jane to someone named Dennis Powells from months before.

> *Hi Jane—I got a package for someone named Marnie Bullock. I think it was just mis-delivered into the big stack of my online orders. Do you want me to drop it at the post office or keep it here for you to pick up?*

Jane had replied that he could drop it off at the post office and let them know it wasn't his. Taylor's thoughts were interrupted by raised voices coming from the kitchen. She paused, hand on her mouse, while she listened.

Lucy's voice, sharp and cutting. Then Anna, firm and defensive.

Taylor was thankful that Cate had rallied her sisters to start coming over and interacting with Lucy, to help get her back on track, but the kids were asleep. The last thing she needed was a full-blown argument waking them.

She quickly set her laptop aside, brushing her hair out of her face as she climbed off the bed and grabbed her cane from where it leaned against the nightstand.

Diesel stood, ready to help if needed.

"Good boy, but I got it." She crossed the hall.

Johnny was napping in Alice's bed, alongside the crib. Taylor peeked in, saw that they were both still sleeping, and gently pulled the door closed.

By the time Taylor reached the kitchen, the tension was thick enough to choke on.

"You need to get back to your life, Lucy," Anna was saying, her arms crossed tightly over her chest. "This—hiding in Taylor's house, pretending the rest of the world doesn't exist—it isn't helping you. You need to go back to work. Get out. Do something."

Lucy shot up from her chair, her hands slamming onto the table. "Oh, so you're an expert on mental health now? Just because you're taking a couple of classes at the community college doesn't mean you're suddenly a mental health expert, Anna, so why don't you keep your opinions to yourself?"

Anna didn't back down, her jaw tightening. "I don't have to be a doctor to know that wallowing like this isn't good for you. You think I don't see what you're doing? You're shutting yourself off. You won't talk to anyone. You barely look at Johnny—"

"Don't you dare," Lucy hissed, her voice trembling. "Don't you dare bring Johnny into this. I take care of my son."

Cate stood up, her calm but commanding presence cutting through the chaos. She walked around the table to Lucy and tried to wrap an arm around her shoulders, but Lucy shrugged her off, pacing toward the window with wild, restless energy.

Taylor lingered in the doorway, torn. She wanted to step in, to take control like she always had. But the words wouldn't come. They were stuck in her throat, tangled and jumbled, her thoughts racing too fast to sort them out, her brain choosing the worst moment to go haywire again.

Jo, still sitting quietly at the table, cleared her throat. "Lucy," she said softly, her voice barely audible, "maybe Anna's right. Just—"

"Don't you start!" Lucy snapped, spinning around to glare at her. "You think you get to weigh in on this, too? You're just as screwed up as I am and I'm pretty sure you've barely left this property in months. You lurk around here like you've done something wrong, so maybe you should see a shrink yourself, sister."

Jo stared back at Lucy, then looked at Taylor for help.

"Lucy, please," Cate said, her voice firm but gentle. "Sit down. You're going to wake the baby."

Lucy threw her hands in the air, her voice rising. "Oh, I know! Because everything is my fault, right? I can't keep Johnny on a routine. I make messes. I can't live alone anymore because I'm the crazy sister! Isn't that what everyone thinks?"

Taylor finally found her voice, stepping into the room. "Lucy, stop. Please. You're not yourself right now."

Lucy turned on her, her eyes blazing. "And what would you know about it, Taylor? You think you can fix me? Fix this family? Well, newsflash—you can't. You never could, and you never will. Everyone acts like it's just me, that they're so solid. But ice is solid, too, until you put a little heat on it."

Taylor blinked, taken aback.

Lucy pressed on, her voice trembling but defiant. "This might be my turn in the fire, but don't think yours isn't coming. And I'm not the only one with secrets."

"Lucy—" Taylor started, but Lucy cut her off, pointing at Anna.

"You think Anna's got it all together? That she's perfect now? She's still binge drinking. She's just hiding it better this time."

"I am not!" Anna's voice cracked like a whip, her face flushing. "I barely ever drink now, and you know it!"

Lucy laughed, a bitter, hollow sound. "Sure. Keep telling yourself that. And Jo?" She turned her attention to her sister, who flinched at the sound of her name. "You all think that Jo's gotten over all her trauma and is just fine? Here's a headline— she's not. She's fighting the urge to off herself every damn day. Just ask her—if you can get past the passive smiles and everything is fine bullshit. But, no, let's all pile on Lucy because she's the easy target, right?"

Jo's face crumpled, tears spilling down her cheeks as she stared out the window, refusing to meet anyone's eyes.

The sound of Lennon crying drifted down the hall, thin and plaintive. Taylor closed her eyes, her head pounding as she squeezed her temples between her fingers.

Johnny shuffled into the kitchen, rubbing his eyes and clutching his stuffed dinosaur. He toddled over to Lucy and wrapped his little arms around her legs. "Mama? What's wrong?"

Lucy didn't even seem to notice him. Her chest was heaving, her face flushed with anger. Cate stepped in, scooping

Johnny up and pressing a kiss to his cheek. "Come on, sweetheart," she murmured, her voice soft and soothing. "Mama is just fine. Let's get you back to bed. We'll turn on a cartoon."

Anna was still seething, her hands clenched into fists. "You're just jealous," she snapped at Lucy. "Jealous that I'm doing something with my life while you're stuck here, pretending you're the victim. You hate that I refused to let my trauma define me, and that I'm following my dream, don't you? You've always been jealous of me."

Lucy scoffed. "Jealous of what? Your overprocessed hair or fake nails? Your creepy ex-husband and uptight lifestyle? Even you finally admitted that you hated it. And following your dream? Give me a break, Anna. You're playing nurse so you can snag you another rich husband at the hospital, while I'm out there building a name for myself in the art world. I don't have to depend on anyone, and I make a lot of money, *Anna*. You think I couldn't pack up and move to New York tomorrow if I didn't want Johnny to be raised around family? If I hadn't stuck around this suffocatingly small town, I'd be a household name by now."

"Then do it!" Anna shot back. "What's stopping you, Ms. Moneybags? You can afford the best nannies, now. Put yourself up in some big skyscraper and have a butler. Then watch your child suffer from self-doubt because he has to grow up without a single relative around him."

"Enough!" Taylor's voice cut through the room like a whip, silencing both of them.

She looked around the room, her gaze sweeping over her sisters. Jo was crying quietly by the window, and Anna and Lucy were staring each other down like boxers in a ring.

"This isn't helping anyone," Taylor said, her voice quieter now but no less firm. "We're sisters. We're supposed to be helping each other, not tearing each other apart."

Lucy crossed her arms, her jaw tight, but she didn't say anything. For a moment, the room was silent except for Jo's muffled sobs and the faint sound of Lennon's cries. Taylor felt her chest tighten, the weight of it all pressing down on her.

She took a deep breath, concentrating on keeping the anger out of her voice. "I'm going to go comfort Lennon, and hopefully get her back to sleep. Sam will be coming in for lunch shortly and I want him to have a peaceful break, so, when I come back in here, I want everyone gone. Even you, Lucy. Go home for an hour or two. Let's all think about how we can support each other, not wage war and chaos. Damn it! Haven't we had enough dysfunction in our lives?"

She turned, hiding the sudden tears as she headed down the hall. Her anger blended into the deep sad feeling that settled over her. How had it come to this? They'd come so far over the past few years, and she thought they'd built a new, firm foundation of family. Now it felt like they were splintering further apart with every word.

She made it to the hallway but, suddenly, her feet didn't want to cooperate. She leaned on her cane and hesitated before trying again.

"Taylor, are you okay?" Cate said, coming out of Alice's room.

Cate looked weird to Taylor. As though she was cloaked in a dark cloud. But the cloud got smaller and smaller until her mother's face was barely a pale dot in midst of the shadows.

And then it all went black.

# Chapter Sixteen

The bell over the door gave a rusty chime as Shane stepped into McPherson's Pawn & Gun. The place reeked of cheap coffee, and the faint buzz of fluorescent lights set his nerves on edge. The store was cramped, the walls lined with glass cases full of pistols and revolvers, shelves of ammo stacked haphazardly in corners. Mounted animal heads stared down at him from above, their lifeless glass eyes somehow mocking his presence.

Behind the counter stood Dale McPherson, a wiry man in his forties with a salt-and-pepper mustache and a cigarette dangling from his lips. He glanced up as Shane entered.

"Morning," Shane said, pulling out his badge and holding it up. "I'm Detective Weaver, here on official business. I need your records for all firearm sales over the last sixty days."

McPherson didn't move, didn't even blink. His gaze flicked to the badge, then back to Shane's face, a slow smirk curling his lips. He took the cigarette from his mouth and tapped the ash onto the floor before wedging it back between his teeth.

"Well, well. What a surprise. The Sheriff's boys gracing my

humble establishment," he drawled, leaning on the counter. "What is it this time? Another witch hunt for one of those evil guns you're always blaming for the world's problems?"

Shane was already tired, already on edge from the morning meeting where Tuffin had strutted around like a rooster, bragging about getting the warrant for Timmons' DNA pushed through. Now this. He exhaled sharply through his nose, struggling to keep his voice even. "This isn't a debate, McPherson. Four people are dead, and the weapon used is still unaccounted for. I need those records. Now."

McPherson snorted, shaking his head as he straightened up. "You lawmen are all the same. Come in here, throwing your weight around, acting like you own the damn place. Let me tell you something, Detective. This is America. You ever heard of the Second Amendment? You know, the one that says folks have the right to bear arms?"

Shane clenched his teeth, his patience slipping through his fingers like sand. "This isn't about the Second Amendment. This is about doing your part to help solve a quadruple homicide. Four innocent people are dead, McPherson. I'm asking for your records because it's my job to make sure the person responsible gets caught before anyone else gets hurt."

McPherson barked out a laugh, the sound sharp and grating. "Oh, sure. And in the meantime, you'd love to shut me down, wouldn't you? You and your kind, always looking for someone to blame. Let me tell you something, fancy boy—guns don't kill people. People kill people. If some jackass takes one of my guns and uses it to shoot up a school or whatever, that's on them, not me."

Shane stepped closer to the counter, his voice dropping to a dangerous level. "You want to talk about responsibility? How about the fact that anyone with a pulse can walk into a shop like this and buy a gun in this state? No permits, no background checks, no nothing. And then when something goes wrong, people like you shrug your shoulders and say, 'Not my problem.'"

McPherson's face reddened, his mustache twitching. "If you don't like the laws, take it up with your governor. He's the one who made it legal for folks to carry a concealed weapon without a license. I don't make the rules—I just follow them."

Shane leaned in, his voice tight with barely contained anger. "The gun laws in this state are a joke, and you know it. That's why we've got tragedies like Apalachee High School—two kids and two teachers gunned down because it's easier to buy an AR-15 than it is to adopt a damn dog."

McPherson's hand slammed down on the counter, rattling the glass cases. "You don't get to come in here and lecture me, boy! I'm running a business. A legal business. You think I'm happy about what happened at that school? You think I like hearing about kids getting shot? But don't you dare stand there and act like it's my fault. You want someone to blame, go look in the damn mirror."

The words hit harder than Shane expected. For a moment, he said nothing, the weight of everything pressing down on him —the dead, the grieving families, the helplessness that came with knowing that the system was rigged against them.

He stepped back, straightening his shoulders.

"I'm not here to argue with you, McPherson," he said, his voice cold and flat. "I'm here to do my job. Now, are you going to give me those records, or am I going to have to get a warrant?"

McPherson glared at him for a long moment, then turned to the computer with a muttered curse. The printer behind him whirred to life, spitting out page after page of sales records. When the last page printed, McPherson grabbed the stack, slammed it down on the counter, and shoved it toward Shane.

"There. Take your damn papers and get out of my store."

Shane picked up the stack, his jaw tight. "Thanks for your cooperation." He turned and walked out, the bell above the door jangling behind him.

He climbed into his truck and tossed the papers onto the passenger seat, his chest heaving with suppressed anger. When he pulled out his phone to check his messages, the email notification was the final straw.

> *Weaver, this is not Taylor. It's Sam. Taylor had a relapse and is in the hospital recovering. Read this carefully: SHE IS OFF THE CASE. Don't email her. Don't call her. Don't text her. Let her rest until she comes back to work.*
> *Signed, HER HUSBAND!*

Shane's hand slammed down on the steering wheel, the sharp sting of pain barely registering. "Damn it, Sam!" he shouted. "You don't know her like I do."

He sat there for a moment, breathing heavily, his thoughts a jumbled mess of frustration and worry. Taylor's relapse wasn't because of the case. It was due to her family, her bloodsucking sisters and the weight of their constant demands.

Sam didn't see that. He didn't understand. He hadn't been around long enough to know how they all did her.

Shane started the truck and peeled out of the gun store parking lot, his hands gripping the wheel so tightly his knuckles turned white. At first, he didn't know where he was going, but the pull was magnetic, irresistible.

He had to see her.

When he pulled into the hospital parking lot and saw Sam's truck, his jaw clenched, his hands resting on the steering wheel as he stared at the doors.

*Damn it.*

Shane wouldn't go in there today. But he'd be back.

# Chapter Seventeen

The first thing Taylor noticed was the beeping. Rhythmic, persistent, and annoyingly close to her ear. She winced, her eyelids heavy as if glued shut. A hand touched her forehead, warm and gentle, smoothing away the damp strands of hair stuck to her skin.

"Taylor?" Cecil's voice was soft, coaxing her back from the darkness. "Come on, sweetheart. Open those beautiful brown eyes for me."

She forced her lids to flutter open, squinting against the harsh white glare of fluorescent lights. The hospital room came into focus slowly, sterile and impersonal, with muted gray walls and a faint antiseptic smell clinging to the air.

"Cecil," she croaked, her voice a hoarse whisper.

"I'm here," he murmured, leaning closer. His dark eyes searched hers, worry etched into every line of his face. "Don't try to talk."

Sam's gruff voice cut through from somewhere to her right. "You scared the hell out of us, Taylor. What were you thinking, letting yourself get so worked up?"

"What—what happened?" she asked, her head throbbing as she tried to piece together the fragments of her memory.

"You collapsed," Cecil said, his hand still stroking her forehead. "Right there in the hallway. They couldn't wake you up."

Sam leaned forward in his chair, his arms crossed over his chest. His jaw was tight, and his eyes burned with anger that barely masked his fear. "The doctor said you pushed your brain too far. You're still recovering from that meningitis, for God's sake, and your sisters decide to have World War Three in our kitchen. And you—" He pointed a finger at her. "You let them."

Taylor winced, her mind rushing back to the kitchen argument. Lucy's accusations, Anna's defensiveness, Jo's quiet sobs. She closed her eyes against the wave of guilt crashing over her. But she hadn't let them, had she? She faintly remembered shutting it down and ordering them out of her house.

"I already told Lucy she had to move out before you come home. And don't worry, Cate and Ellis talked her into staying with Jo and Levi, until her therapist thinks she's ready to live alone again."

"The kids," she whispered. "Lennon and Johnny—are they okay?"

"They're fine," Cecil assured her quickly. "Cate has them. Lennon's with her right now, and Johnny's playing with his toy trucks. Alice is helping watch out for them. They're safe."

Taylor's chest tightened. "How long have I been out? Lennon needs to nurse."

Sam sighed, running a hand through his hair. "You've been asleep for about six hours. The doctor recommended a formula for now, just until you're strong enough to handle everything again. Cate's got it covered."

Taylor's throat tightened with emotion. "She needs *me*," she said, tears welling up in her eyes. "Not *manufactured* milk."

"You're right, she needs a healthy mom," Sam said firmly.

"And right now, that means resting and letting people help you. Don't argue with me on this, Taylor. You're not invincible."

Before Taylor could respond, the door opened, and Dr. Kellner walked in, his white coat pristine and his expression professional but kind.

"Good to see you awake, Taylor," he said, pulling up a stool beside her bed. "How are you feeling?"

"Like I got hit by a truck," she admitted.

He nodded. "That's to be expected. Your brain's been through a lot these past few months and, today, it essentially hit a wall. The stress, combined with your ongoing recovery, caused a temporary shutdown. It's your body's way of forcing you to rest when you won't do it yourself."

Taylor frowned. "So what now? Can I go home?"

Dr. Kellner smiled faintly, but there was no mistaking the firmness in his tone. "I'd like you to stay for at least another day so we can monitor you. Make sure there's no lingering neurological impact. And after that, I want you to seriously consider scaling back. Whatever's on your plate right now—it can wait."

Taylor thought about the Colburns, and the person who had killed them, yet unnamed or brought to justice. She glanced at Sam and Cecil, her cheeks burning with shame. "I have a lot to do," she protested.

Sam seemed to read her mind. "Like Shane's emails about that case? Yeah, I saw your laptop open when we got home. You're pushing yourself too hard, Taylor, and it's going to kill you if you don't stop."

Taylor looked away, her guilt deepening. "I just ... I can't sit back and do nothing. People are counting on me."

Cecil's hand tightened around hers. "Taylor, you don't have to carry the weight of the world on your shoulders. It's okay to let go sometimes. To focus on yourself."

The doctor's expression softened. "He's right. And you

need to understand something: people having difficult feelings is not an emergency. You don't have to swoop in and fix everything the second someone's upset. That's not your job."

"Amen to that," Sam said.

Taylor's lips trembled. She thought about how things used to be, with her family barely talking or seeing each other. She didn't want to lose what they had now and go back to that. "But if I don't, who will?"

Cecil leaned closer, his voice gentle but firm. "Taylor, it takes practice to let go of that instinct. To realize that it's not your responsibility to solve everyone's problems. Sometimes, just being there is enough."

Dr. Kellner nodded in agreement. "And in your case, putting your health first isn't selfish—it's necessary. If you don't take care of yourself, you can't take care of anyone else. Especially that beautiful baby girl."

Taylor swallowed hard, her tears finally spilling over. She already missed Lennon so much that it hurt. But the thoughts about her sisters tumbled over and over in her mind. The worry and frustration. "I don't know how to stop," she admitted, her voice breaking.

Sam reached out, his hand resting on her shoulder. "You'll learn. But first, you've got to give yourself the chance to heal. Promise me you'll try, Taylor. For Lennon, for Alice, for all of us. If you think your family can't survive without you, then you should put yourself at the top of the priority list."

She nodded slowly, her heart heavy but her resolve beginning to form. "I'll try," she whispered.

# Chapter Eighteen

Shane pulled up a long driveway, dust kicking up around his truck as he parked near the barn. The property was to the west of Cotton Timmons and belonged to Robert Gilley, a retired forester known for his straightforward demeanor and love of horses. Shane had met Gilley a few times over the years.

Deputy Kuno had already questioned him, but Shane wanted more.

The barn doors were open, revealing a tidy interior with tools hanging neatly on the walls and a chestnut horse tethered in the center aisle. Gilley stood beside the horse, brushing its coat in slow, deliberate strokes.

"Deputy Weaver," Gilley said with a nod when Shane stepped inside. "What brings you out here?"

Shane approached, removing his hat. "Morning, Mr. Gilley. I know you've already given a statement that you heard nothing the day of the crimes, but I'm here about your neighbor—Cotton Timmons."

Gilley's hand paused mid-stroke before resuming. "Figures. He finally done something stupid enough to land him in jail?"

Shane cracked a slight smile but quickly sobered. "Not yet, but his name keeps coming up. I wanted to ask if you've had any dealings with him."

Gilley let out a low whistle. "Dealings? Hell, Deputy, I've had more than my share of dealings with Cotton. Man's got a temper that burns hotter than a blister bug in a pepper patch."

"Go on," Shane prompted.

Gilley leaned against the horse, crossing his arms. "Ol' Cotton thinks his property is the holy land. Couple years back, we had a big dust-up over the property line. Cotton swore up and down that some of my fence posts were on his side. I told him he was full of it, but he kept coming over, yelling about it and insisting he was right. Then one day, he showed up with a shotgun slung over his shoulder, telling me I'd better move my fence or else."

Shane's stomach tightened. "He threatened you?"

"Sure did," Gilley said, his tone calm but firm. "Told me he'd 'handle it his own way' if I didn't fix it. I didn't take kindly to that, but I'm a calm man. One that don't go shooting off his mouth without facts to back it up. So I hired a surveyor. Turns out the fence was smack dab where it should've been. Cotton was wrong."

"What happened after that?" Shane asked.

"Not much. I showed him the survey report, and he huffed and puffed but didn't apologize. We haven't spoken since. He keeps to his side of the line, and I keep to mine."

"Sounds like you're better off that way," Shane said.

"You're not wrong," Gilley replied, brushing his horse again. "Cotton's always been that way—stubborn as a mule and mean as a snake when he thinks he's been crossed. He's one of the sorry crop who show up at all the town council meetings, complaining about crap that can't be changed instead of focusing on what can be."

129

"What about his family?" Shane asked.

Gilley snorted. "What family? His wife left him years ago. Couldn't put up with him anymore and got out of Georgia. Took the kids with her. From what I hear, they're all grown and scattered across South Carolina now. Don't think they keep in touch. Can't blame 'em, either."

Shane nodded thoughtfully. "So he's been living alone all this time?"

"Yep. Just him, his pitiful dog, and his grievances. Man's got nothing but time to stew in his own bitterness."

"Has he ever mentioned the Colburns to you?" Shane pressed.

Gilley shook his head. "Not directly, but I've heard down at the barber shop that he's going around griping about their dog a time or two. Said it was running loose and getting into his chickens. Don't know if there's any truth to it, but Cotton doesn't let things go easy. If he's got a grudge, he'll carry it to the grave."

*Or to someone else's graves.*

Shane thanked Gilley and made his way back to his SUV, his mind churning. The property line dispute and past threat of violence gave him a clearer picture of Timmons' temper. Combined with his ongoing feud with the Colburns, it was more than enough to keep the man in his sights.

The next stop was Cotton Timmons' property. His old pickup truck was parked out front. As Shane stepped out of his vehicle, the screen door banged open, and Cotton stomped onto the porch, his face red with anger.

"Deputy, I've about had it with y'all," Cotton growled, jabbing a finger toward Shane. "Them GBI folks were here yesterday, poking around, taking my damn DNA like I'm some kind of criminal. I've done nothing wrong, and I'm sick of being treated like this. I've got rights and y'all are breaking them!"

Shane held up a calming hand. "Mr. Timmons, calm down.

I'm here to follow up, that's all. And for the record, I'm not a deputy. It's *Detective* Weaver. I've got a few more questions, and then I'll be on my way."

Cotton crossed his arms, glaring. "You'd better make it quick. I've had enough of this nonsense."

Shane's eyes drifted past Cotton to the battered suitcases stacked just inside the doorway. "Going somewhere?"

"Yeah," Cotton snapped. "Like I told your guy Tuffin, it's my annual fishing trip in Colorado. I've been planning it for months, and I'll be damned if I'm letting you or anyone else stop me."

Shane's brow arched. "Convenient timing."

"Don't you start," Cotton barked. "I've got nothing to hide, and I'm tired of y'all harassing me. This is the last time I'm answering questions. Next time, I'm calling a lawyer."

Shane stepped onto the porch, his tone steady. "Then let's make this quick. About the Colburns—have you ever, at any time, been inside their home?"

"Nope. Unlike you and your people, I respect a man's home as his personal property. We ain't friends and there's no reason I would've been inside." Cotton crossed his arms over his chest and leaned against the porch pole.

"Okay," Shane said. "Next. You said their dog was on your property, killing your chickens. Do you have proof of that?"

"I got a photo of the dog standing right near where my chickens roost," Cotton said, his voice rising. "That's proof enough!"

"Was the dog barking? Chasing? Acting aggressive?"

"No, not while I was looking but that don't mean nothing," Cotton snapped. "And what does it matter now? The Colburns are dead, so there's no more feud."

Shane tilted his head, studying Cotton. "Seems like a lot of anger over something pretty small, don't you think?"

Cotton bristled. "I've got every right to be angry. Folks need to keep their animals on their own property. Dogs run off deer I want to hunt, kill livestock, tear up gardens. You'd be mad, too, if it was your land."

"And what about the dog excrement in the Colburns' mailbox last year?" Shane asked.

Cotton's face darkened. "I told Willis, that wasn't me. I ain't bagging up no dog shit for any reason no matter how mad I am."

"Would you take a polygraph to prove that?" Shane pressed.

Cotton's eyes narrowed, and he stepped back, gripping the edge of the door. "This conversation's over. I'm getting a lawyer."

The door slammed shut, and Shane stood on the porch for a moment, his jaw tightening. Cotton Timmons was hiding something—he was sure of it. Now, it was just a matter of finding out what.

# Chapter Nineteen

F riday morning Taylor sat cross-legged on the hospital bed, fully dressed in her street clothes as her hands rested lightly in her lap. Dr. Merrow settled into the chair beside her. The psychologist had a calm, steady presence, her voice measured and gentle as she spoke.

"Dr. Kellner asked that I stop by and do an evaluation, Taylor. I've heard that you've had a rough couple of days," Dr. Merrow began, her pen poised over a notepad. "How are you feeling now?"

"Better," Taylor replied, her voice soft. It wasn't a lie, exactly, but it wasn't the full truth either. Her body felt steadier, her mind a little clearer, but the swirling emotions were still there, just beneath the surface. Worry. So much worry about everyone.

Especially Lennon. She had to get back to her baby. Sam had offered to bring her to visit, but Taylor hadn't wanted to expose her to any hospital germs or illnesses floating around. Her breasts throbbed, needing to connect with her child. To nurture and protect her.

Dr. Merrow nodded, studying her carefully. "You've been in

crisis mode for a long time, haven't you? Even before your recent illness."

Taylor hesitated, the words striking uncomfortably close to home. "I guess you could say that. I mean, it comes and goes but for, sure, getting so sick put a damper on the last few months."

"I think we both know it's more than that," the psychologist said. "Sam filled me in a bit about your background, and what I want you to understand is that when someone is constantly in the role of caregiver, they can lose sight of their own needs. They become so focused on fixing others that they forget how to take care of themselves. Does that resonate with you?"

Taylor shrugged, averting her gaze. "Maybe."

Dr. Merrow leaned forward slightly, her expression kind but firm. "Taylor, I'm not here to judge you, but I need to understand whether you're ready to go home. Whether you're in a place where you can actually take care of yourself. Where you can set boundaries that you need to set."

Taylor swallowed hard, her throat tightening. She was leaving the hospital with or without her doctor's approval. Two days was enough, and she didn't care what they said. Sam was already on his way, too. "I can handle it. I always do."

"But that's part of the problem," Dr. Merrow said. "You're handling things, but at what cost? Burnout, resentment, denying your own needs—those are all signs of someone who's stretched too thin. It's okay to admit that you need help. That doesn't make you weak; it makes you human."

The words hit like a hammer, cracking open a part of her she'd tried to keep sealed. But before she could respond, a knock at the door interrupted them.

Dr. Merrow glanced at Taylor, then stood to open the door. Shane stood there, holding a bouquet of flowers wrapped in cheap plastic from the hospital gift shop.

He looked uncomfortable, shifting his weight from one foot to the other.

"Hi. I—I'm Detective Weaver, a colleague of Taylor's." He looked around Merrow and waved at Taylor.

"Detective Weaver," Dr. Merrow said, a note of surprise in her voice. "We're in the middle of a session. Can you come back later?"

"Sorry," Shane said, though he didn't look it. "I just wanted to check on her. I'll wait outside."

Taylor sighed, already feeling the tension creeping back into her chest. She needed to get rid of him before Sam showed up to take her home. "It's fine. You can come in."

Dr. Merrow hesitated, then nodded. "Alright, but we're going to finish this conversation before your discharge." She turned to Shane. "Please be mindful of her recovery. She's been through a lot."

"I understand," Shane said, stepping into the room as the psychologist left. He set the flowers on the bedside table and sat in the chair Dr. Merrow had vacated.

Taylor glanced at the flowers, then back at him. "You didn't have to do that."

"I wanted to," he said simply. "How are you feeling?"

"Like I need to go home," she said with a small smile. "But they're making me jump through hoops to earn my walking papers. What's going on with the case? Any big leads?"

He shook his head, his expression serious. "Nothing major but we're making progress. Got the warrant for Timmons' DNA, and we have a few more people to interview. It's not much, but it's something."

"That's good," she said, though her voice lacked enthusiasm. She thought of Sam and hesitated, then added, "Shane, I need to step back from this. I know I wasn't doing much, but I can't ... I can't keep adding to my plate right now."

Shane's jaw tightened, but he nodded. "Don't forget, you asked me to let you help. But it's not the job that's wearing you down, Taylor. It's everything else. Your family ... they're draining you."

Her stomach twisted, and she shifted uncomfortably. "Shane—"

"No, hear me out," he interrupted. "Lucy and Anna—they use you. They take and take, and they don't give anything back. And Sam—" He stopped himself, his frustration evident. "Since you married him, you've been different. Like you're trying to be someone you're not. He forgets that you were already something special before he came along. You're damn good at your job, and you have a bright future in—"

Taylor held her hand up to stop him. Her irritation flared, and she sat up straighter. "Don't talk about my husband like that. Sam is the only thing that keeps me grounded. You don't know what you're talking about."

Shane's face darkened, a flash of something unreadable in his eyes. "I just think you deserve better," he muttered.

Before she could respond, a movement in the doorway caught her eye. She looked up to see Sam standing there, his face a mask of fury. She sensed an impending disaster in three, two, one ...

He strode into the room, his gaze locked on Shane. "Get out," he said, his voice low and dangerous.

"Sam, wait—" she started, but it was too late. She leaped from the bed, trying to head off what was coming. She didn't get into the middle fast enough before Sam grabbed Shane by the arm and yanked him out of the chair. Shane shoved him back, his expression hardening. "You want to do this here, Sam?" he said, his voice like ice.

"Maybe I do," Sam shot back, his voice rising. "Why the hell are you here? Bringing flowers like you're some kind of savior? Taylor is my wife. My responsibility."

"You don't own her," Shane snapped, shoving Sam back. "And you sure as hell don't understand her."

The tension exploded as Sam swung, his fist connecting with Shane's jaw. Shane staggered but recovered quickly, throwing a punch of his own. Taylor screamed for them to stop, but they were already in the hallway, grappling like two bulls locked in a fight.

"Enough!" she shouted, her voice hoarse with anger.

Nurses screamed and a pair of doctors rushed in, pulling the two men apart. One of them glared at both of them. "If you don't leave right now, I'm calling the police."

"I *am* the police," Shane snapped, wiping blood from his lip.

"Then act like it," the doctor shot back.

Sam glared at Shane, his chest heaving. "You're a damn joke," he spat. "Stay away from my wife."

"Both of you, out," Taylor said, her voice cold and furious. She pointed to the door. "Sam, I'll meet you in the car. Now."

Sam hesitated, his face still red with anger, but eventually he turned and stormed out. Shane lingered for a moment, his gaze meeting Taylor's, something unspoken passing between them. Then he, too, walked away.

As the door clicked shut, Taylor sank back onto the bed, her head pounding.

What just happened?

Her hands trembled as she reached for the flowers, then shoved them off the table. They landed on the floor with a muted thud, petals scattering across the tiles.

She closed her eyes, her breath shaky. "What the hell is wrong with everyone?" she muttered to herself. But deep down, she knew the answer wasn't as simple as blaming them. Something had to change—starting with her.

# Chapter Twenty

Monday was not starting off well for Shane because sporting a shiner for the update meeting with Dawkins and the GBI duo was the last thing he wanted to do. Wearing sunglasses indoors would make it worse, so he was going to have to listen to rousting about it all day.

He successfully avoided anyone in the hallway and was the first into the conference room, looking down at his notes when the door swung open, and the other three filed in and took a seat.

"Morning, Weaver," Sheriff Dawkins said.

"Good morning." Shane didn't look up. He doodled in the margin of his legal pad.

Tuffin and Hanson didn't bother with niceties. They were well aware of Shane's resistance to working with them.

"What's new?" Dawkins asked. "Give me something, y'all."

Shane finally looked up. "I'm focusing on Cotton Timmons right now. I talked to the neighbor on the other side of him and he says Timmons has an explosive temper. Threatened to kill him a year or so ago over property lines."

Dawkins nodded. "Whoa. Hold on about Timmons for a minute. First, let's talk about how you got that black eye."

"That's proprietary information and not related to the case."

"It damn well better not be," Dawkins said. "Go on."

Shane ran his hand through his hair, obliterating the perfection of the style he'd left it in when he arrived at work. "I ran him, and it appears that he's got a record. He was arrested on cruelty to children and false imprisonment and got off with two years' probation. The crime was against his wife at the time for the imprisonment, and his own children for excessive punishment."

The sheriff's phone rang, and he looked at it, then excused himself to take the call outside the room. The door slammed behind him.

"Excessively punishing your children and refusing to let your wife leave is a far cry from committing mass murder," Tuffin said. "Hell, these days you even yell at your child and someone is calling it abuse. And side note, why did we waste time on a warrant for his DNA if he was already in the system? Sounds like an amateur mistake."

"His DNA wasn't in the system, Tuffin," Shane said, his tone even and deadly. "He didn't do any time, and his felony was before legislature expanded the database to include certain felony probationers. But speaking of DNA, I thought your team was going to put a rush on DNA collected from the scene? I haven't heard a thing."

They stared at each other, a silent challenge.

Hanson finally broke in. "Is this some kind of pissing contest because, last I heard, we're supposed to be a team. Grow up, boys." Her lips pressed into a line so fine they were nearly invisible.

Dawkins returned and looked around before sitting.

"What did I miss?"

"Nothing, sir," Tuffin said.

Shane continued, but kept his gaze on the sheriff, refusing to look at Tuffin again. "Rumor has it that someone left a bag of dog manure in the Colburns mailbox last year, and the eldest daughter, Missy Ann, says they all believed it came from Timmons. Willis Colburn threatened to have him arrested if he could prove it, but nothing came of it."

"Probably teenagers having fun on a Friday night," Tuffin said, rolling his eyes sarcastically toward the ceiling.

"Awful coincidental that it happens during a neighbor spat about a dog crossing over property lines, don't you think?" Shane asked.

"Did you get his DNA, Tuffin?" Dawkins asked.

"Yes, we did," he said, lifting his chin proudly.

"Okay, well, when the forensics come back, we'll see if he pops up in the crime scene," Dawkins said.

"If he does, we'd better hope he comes back because right now he's over fifteen hundred miles away, somewhere in Colorado," Shane said, then looked straight at Tuffin. "He said he made you aware."

"Well, shit," Hanson said, sighing her exasperation.

"Why did we let him leave?" Dawkins said to Tuffin.

"We've no reason to hold him, that's why," he said. "Anyway, he's not our guy."

Shane's eyebrows shot up. "Why is that, Sherlock?"

"If Timmons had done this, he wouldn't have been sitting around his house waiting on us to show up. He'd have run weeks ago to get a head start."

"Unless he thought he left things so clean we couldn't pin it on him," Shane said. "By the time the bodies were found, Timmons had sufficient time to clean himself up and get back home through their joined properties without setting foot anywhere anyone else could see him. He also has about forty acres in which to hide a weapon. Now that we pressed him for his DNA, he's got a fishing trip all the way across the country. That's convenient."

"Guys—" Dawkins said, holding his hand up. "Nothing we can do yet on him. So what else do we have?"

Hanson tapped her pen on the table as she read off her notes. "I went through all the public records for Willis and Jane, looking through properties they've bought and sold. Their current land is the only one they've purchased in over a decade. Before that, it was a small place on the other side of town but looks like a clean sale."

Shane held in his exasperation.

Dawkins leaned back in his chair, his fingers steepled as he absorbed the updates. "Alright, we've got Timmons out of town, but his DNAs on the way. What about Missy Ann Colburn? Anything else we can dig into?"

"Missy Ann lives in the Atlanta suburbs with her son, Justin," Shane said. "She's been divorced for about four years now. She interviewed before and after the funeral, answering all my questions when asked. Claims she hasn't been back to the family property in over six months. Said she has a strong relationship with her parents but has been busy managing her career and raising Justin. She's a pharmaceutical rep and travels a lot for work."

"Anything unusual in her background?" Dawkins asked.

Shane shook his head. "Nothing glaring. Financials are stable, no criminal record. Her social media's pretty clean— mostly pictures of her and Justin, work events, and a few with friends. She's kept a relatively low profile online."

"What about her ex-husband?" Dawkins pressed. "Justin's father. Could there be bad blood there?"

Shane glanced back down at his notes. "Thomas 'Tommy' Pratt. Works in construction, owns a small remodeling business out near Ellijay—not too far from Jasper. Their divorce was finalized about four years ago, and there's no indication of any custody battles—seems like they've kept things civil for Justin's sake. That said, I did some digging, and Tommy had some financial trouble a while back. A couple of lawsuits from dissatisfied clients, though nothing criminal. The timing of the divorce and the lawsuits overlap, so maybe it put some strain on the marriage."

"What about his relationship with the Colburns?" Dawkins asked.

"Hard to say. Missy Ann mentioned her parents adored Justin and were always there for her during and after the divorce, but she didn't bring up Tommy much. Could be worth asking if there were any tensions. Maybe he felt like they sided with her, or there was some falling out we don't know about."

Shane thought of something else and interjected, flipping a page in his file. "Hey— this might be worth noting: Seth Colburn was also in construction. Did a lot of contracting work out of Jasper. It's possible he and Tommy Pratt crossed paths— maybe even worked on a job together."

Dawkins raised an eyebrow. "You think there could've been bad blood between them?"

"Could be," Shane said, leaning back in his chair. "Small-town construction is a tight-knit business, and disputes over clients or contracts can get ugly. If Seth and Tommy had a falling out, it might've created tension in the family. We need to see if there's any record of them working together—or any legal disputes that might have come out of it."

"Good point," Dawkins said, nodding. "Follow that thread. Check for any business connections between Seth and Tommy. If there's a history there, it could give us a new angle."

"I already ran his address," Shane said, closing his notebook.

"Tommy Pratt's maybe forty-five minutes from here. I'm headed there now."

"Hold on," Tuffin cut in. "We'll handle this. No sense in you wasting your time driving out there when we can—"

"No," Shane interrupted sharply, standing up and grabbing his coat. "I'm on it."

"Weaver—" Tuffin started, but Shane was already heading for the door.

Before anyone could argue further, Shane stormed out, slamming the door behind him. The sound echoed in the room as the others exchanged glances.

"Well," Tuffin muttered. "That was mature."

"Let him go," Dawkins said with a resigned sigh. "If he's that determined, maybe he'll get something out of the guy."

# Chapter Twenty-One

The rhythmic hum of his SUV's tires against the cold asphalt was the only sound keeping Shane company as he drove through the winding roads that led from sheriff's headquarters to Ellijay. A radio blasting in the cab would've only added to his stress. The drive wasn't long, but it was quiet and that gave him enough time to replay everything he'd pieced together so far.

He planned on talking to Missy Ann again to ask her about her ex and get her take on whether he had any beef with her family. He was angry at himself that he hadn't thought to ask her that in the other interviews, though she had put him off by saying she'd been divorced for years, and it hadn't been contentious. Still, he'd dropped that thread too soon. Made him look stupid in front of Dawkins and Tuffin. He should've let them do the follow up, but he couldn't shake the nagging feeling that if he let Tuffin or Hanson chase this lead and they cracked the case while he was spinning his wheels on someone else, it'd be a blow to both his pride and his standing in the department.

His gut still told him Cotton Timmons was the better suspect. The man had a documented history of violence, and the neighbor had painted him as someone with a volatile temper. He had easy access to the property, and motive.

Shane tightened his grip on the steering wheel, thinking hard.

Thomas Pratt was a long shot, no doubt about it, but long shots had a way of turning into wins if you hit the right target. He went over what he knew: the divorce, the financial troubles, and just what if—a possible tension with Seth?—it was enough to raise questions, and he should've been on it.

As the mountain roads stretched out before him, Shane's mind wandered back to Seth. According to everyone who knew him, the man had been a talented carpenter, steady and hard-working. If Seth had worked under Pratt when he was starting out, there could've been tensions, right?

Pratt's address came into view as Shane turned down a quiet, gravel road that led to a small ranch-style home. The place was modest but well-kept, with a fenced-in yard and a few toys scattered near the porch—evidence of a child who lived there. As Shane pulled up and parked, a dog started barking from somewhere inside the house.

He stepped out of the truck, the crunch of gravel under his boots announcing his arrival. Before he could knock, the front door opened, and a woman holding a toddler on her hip appeared. The dog, a wiry terrier mix, hovered at her feet, barking loudly.

"Can I help you?" she asked, her expression guarded.

"Ma'am, I'm Detective Weaver from Hart's Ridge," he said, pulling his badge from his coat pocket. "I'm looking for Tommy Pratt. Is he home?"

She shifted the toddler to her other hip and tightened her grip on the doorframe. "No, he's at work."

"Mind if I come in?" Shane asked, though he already knew the answer.

"I do, actually," she said, her tone firm. "Tommy didn't do anything wrong, and I don't want my son getting scared by whatever this is about."

Shane nodded, recognizing that she wasn't going to budge. "Fair enough. Can you tell me where he's working?"

She hesitated, glancing back into the house before answering. "He's at a remodel on Chestnut Hollow. Just past the fork in the road, you'll see a white truck and a dumpster out front."

"Thank you, ma'am," Shane said, tipping his head slightly before stepping back to his vehicle. The dog's barking followed him as he drove off.

The remodel site wasn't hard to find. It was a two-story farmhouse undergoing extensive work, with a crew scattered across the property. Power tools buzzed, and the faint smell of sawdust filled the air. Shane spotted a man who matched Pratt's description: tall, broad-shouldered, wearing a faded ball cap and a toolbelt slung low over his hips. He was directing two younger men who were carrying a heavy beam toward the porch.

Shane stepped out of his truck and approached. "Tommy Pratt?"

Pratt turned, squinting against the sun. "Yeah, who's asking?"

"Detective Shane Weaver. I need a few minutes of your time."

Pratt scowled and glanced at the beam his crew was struggling with. "Can't this wait? As you can see, I'm in the middle of something here."

"Afraid not," Shane said, crossing his arms. "But I'll keep it short."

With a sigh, Pratt waved the crew off and stepped closer. "Alright, what's this about?"

Shane didn't waste time. "I'm looking into the murders of the Colburn family. Your ex-wife's family."

Pratt stiffened slightly, then folded his arms across his chest. "I already heard about it. Terrible thing. But other than getting my son one weekend a month, I haven't had anything to do with Missy Ann or her family in years, so, if you're here to pin this on me, you're wasting your time."

"Relax," Shane said. "Just trying to connect some dots. I hear you knew Seth Colburn pretty well."

Pratt nodded slowly. "I did. Hell, I taught the kid a lot of what he knows—or knew, I guess. Missy Ann pushed him on me, so he worked for me for a few years when he was starting out. Damn fine carpenter. Sharp, too. Picked things up quick."

"So why'd he leave?" Shane asked, watching Pratt closely.

Pratt shrugged, but there was tension in the movement. "He wanted to strike out on his own. Can't blame him for that. Kid had natural talent, and he wasn't gonna waste it working for someone else forever."

"Any hard feelings about that?" Shane pressed. He knew that no business owner enjoyed losing a good employee, especially one who could turn into competition.

Pratt's jaw tightened. "Look, nobody likes losing good help, alright? But Seth and I parted on good terms. I wished him nothing but the best. I've even recommended him for jobs I didn't have the time to take on. Far as I know, he was doing fine for himself."

"Okay," Shane said, keeping his tone neutral. "What about Missy Ann? Any issues between you and her family during or after the divorce?"

"None worth mentioning," Pratt said. "Did she send you here to talk to me? I'd be surprised if she did. Willis and Jane were good people. Loved their grandson, treated me fine. Whatever happened between me and Missy Ann, it didn't spill over to them. We kept our divorce friendly. For our son, really, but we didn't want to have anyone taking sides."

Shane let the silence hang for a moment before asking, "Would you be willing to give a DNA sample? Just to eliminate yourself as a suspect."

Pratt's eyes flickered with hesitation. "What? You want me to give you my DNA just like that?"

"It's standard procedure," Shane said, his voice firm but not unkind. "If you've got nothing to hide, it'll clear you. If not, I'll just have to keep looking into it. Saves both of us time."

Pratt glared at him for a moment, then let out a breath. "Fine. If it'll get you off my back. I've got a deadline to finish this house, and I don't want to be dragged into an investigation that's going to keep me offsite. I'll do it, but I don't like it."

Shane didn't acknowledge the comment. "Appreciate it. I'll have someone come by for the sample. Tomorrow work?"

Pratt muttered something under his breath, then turned to his crew, already barking orders. Shane filed away the brief interaction, noting the way Pratt had been quick to agree, but still bristled at the request. There was something off about that. It wasn't typical for someone innocent to act that way.

Shane didn't linger long. "Appreciate your time, Pratt. I'll let you get back to it."

Pratt didn't reply, already deep into directing orders again.

Shane climbed into his SUV and drove away, the gears in his head still turning. The answers hadn't been as clear-cut as he hoped, but they'd been revealing in their own way.

# Chapter Twenty-Two

Taylor stood at the sink, one hand on the counter and the other gripping the smooth curve of the cane she'd gotten for Christmas. She glared at it as if it were a personal affront to her independence.

Mondays used to be her busiest days between her own work at the department and everything needing to be done for boarding at the farm. Many of their clients were weekend stays and the check out on Mondays could at times be frantic. Anna was no doubt handling it like a champ though.

A pile of dirty dishes in the sink stared back at Taylor and she felt overwhelmed.

She needed air. And space.

"What's for dinner?" Alice said, coming up behind her.

"I—I'm not sure yet."

"Dad said he's hoping for country-fried steak and taters. But he said he'll fry the meat if I peel potatoes. He doesn't want you stressing over it."

The thought of frying anything made Taylor feel nauseous, but she wasn't letting Sam cook his own meal after working all day. Long gone were the stack of casseroles in the freezer from people like Della Ray and Mabel. Even if they weren't gone, Taylor didn't think her family could stomach even one more casserole, for a very long time. "I can handle dinner. But hey— can you listen for Lennon in case she wakes up early? I need to step outside for a few minutes."

"Yep," Alice said. "I was going in there anyway to lay on my bed and read."

"Thanks, honey." She grabbed her jacket and, using her cane, stepped out on the porch. Diesel joined her before she shut the door, his tail wagging frantically as he ran ahead.

The cool morning air wrapped around Taylor like a reminder of everything she'd been missing—freedom, movement, her life. She walked along, slowly ambling toward the main building.

Diesel stopped and looked back, his dark coat gleaming in the sunlight. He scanned her face, as if he sensed her frustration.

"Don't look at me like that," she muttered. Diesel tilted his head, then ran back and gave her leg a soft nudge with his nose, his way of encouraging her.

He was probably glad just to have her out of the house with him.

Her first stop was the boarding facility. Inside the facility, the energy was palpable. Dogs barked, tails wagged, and the faint scent of shampoo lingered in the air. In the central play corral, a group of dogs—ranging from a sprightly terrier to a lumbering Great Dane—chased each other in chaotic delight. Jo was tossing a ball to a Pomeranian who bounced excitedly nearby, waiting for the release.

Anna stood behind the counter, checking out a woman dressed in head-to-toe designer athleisure, with perfectly coiffed blonde hair and a white poodle in her arms.

The woman's voice was both high-pitched and overly

dramatic. She was in the class of dog-owners that everyone dreaded to see coming.

"How did Mars do with his separation anxiety?" the woman was asking, drawing out the words as though each syllable carried the weight of the world. "He looks skinnier, but I know he won't eat unless the kibble is warmed to precisely room temperature—not a degree more or less, mind you. Did they warm it up first? And what about the topper I sent? It's pure venison crumbles. You know, I tip generously in anticipation of those little touches ..."

Taylor couldn't help herself. She ducked her head behind the woman's back and made an exaggerated wide-eyed face at Anna, silently mouthing *poor darling*.

Anna caught the look and barely held in a laugh, turning her head quickly to hide her smile.

"Yes, and he ate just fine," Anna said smoothly, her professional tone never faltering. "It's not uncommon for a pet to lose a pound or two when their person is away. It's just normal stress. And to be honest, Mars could stand to lose a few more but he did very well here."

Taylor decided to leave Anna to the poodle drama and wandered past the reception desk. Diesel stayed at her side, his nails clicking softly against the polished floors.

She made her way down the row of kennels, stopping to read the names and notes attached to the clipboards at each kennel that contained a guest. The 'suites' were spotless, each outfitted with plush bedding, toys, and stainless-steel bowls.

"Snickers," she read aloud from one clipboard. "Loves belly rubs, hates loud noises. Got it." She moved to the next kennel. "Zelda. Needs slow introductions to new dogs. Good girl, Zelda."

When she reached the Comfort Suites, her chest swelled with pride.

These kennels were the latest additions—a high-end touch for the facility's most pampered guests and probably where Mars had spent the weekend. Each suite was immaculate. Not only that, but these contained soundproof glass doors, luxury lifted beds, and sleek indoor/outdoor spaces with heating and air conditioning.

Everything about them spoke of indulgence. Crazy enough, even in their small, country town, the Comfort Suites were usually booked out far in advance.

She peered into one of them and smiled. Inside were two familiar (and elderly) bulldogs, snuggled together on a fleece blanket. The sign on their door read: Bert and Ernie—senior duo, deaf and incontinent, extra snuggles recommended.

"Hey, boys," Taylor said softly as she opened the door and stepped inside. Diesel waited just outside, his tail wagging as he peeked in. The bulldogs immediately perked up, their heavy breathing filling the room as they waddled over to greet her.

"You two are living the high life with us again, huh?" Taylor said, crouching down to scratch behind their ears. Bert licked her hand while Ernie leaned his weight into her leg, his drool threatening to soak her jeans. "I bet you're the VIPs of the week, aren't you?"

After a few minutes, she reluctantly said goodbye to the bulldogs and headed back to the front. The poodle lady was gone, and Anna was updating the day's schedule on the computer. Jo had left the play area and stood there with her, one hand on her hip.

"Whatcha doing here?" Jo asked.

"Just stopping by for a minute. How's our littlest sister doing?" Taylor asked.

Jo scoffed. "Um—when do you think she'll be ready to move back into her own place?"

So This is Christmas

"That bad, huh?" Anna asked, laughing. "Better you than me. I guess sometimes it pays to be the least liked of the group."

"Stop—" Taylor said. "You are not."

"With Lucy, I am. Not that I care," Anna replied, smiling. "It's a badge I've worn with pride for many years."

Jo laughed.

Taylor didn't. She hated discord between her sisters. "Okay. Whatever. Anyway, Jo, can you tell if she's started answering work calls or emails again? It's not like Lucy to miss a chance to make a dollar. I think that worries me more than anything."

"I've seen her using her phone, but not sure what she's doing on it. She spends a lot of time watching old seasons of Real Housewives, for the most part. She hasn't mentioned mice in, hmmm ... let's see ..." she looked at her phone screen. "Maybe twenty-four hours now."

"I guess that's good," Taylor said, shrugging. "That's better than she was doing at my house. I might check in with her later. As for now, I know Mondays are crazy. Anything I can do to help?"

Anna turned to her with a raised brow. "Nope. I've got strict orders to turn you away if you show up. Go home, Taylor. You need to rest."

"I'm fine," she replied, though the sudden ache in her head begged to differ. Any exertion started up a headache and she was so tired of dealing with it.

"Go. Home." Jo crossed her arms, her expression softening. "I know you're bored, but, really, we've got things under control here."

Taylor sighed, feeling the weight of uselessness settle in her chest. Without another word, she turned and walked out, Diesel trailing faithfully at her side.

She wasn't ready to go home and a quick look at her phone screen showed no messages, meaning Lennon was just fine. She

153

considered stopping by Jo's cabin to check in on Lucy, but decided she didn't have the mental energy for it. Instead, she headed toward the barn.

Inside, the earthy scent of hay and the faint bark of rescue dogs greeted her. Cecil was near the kennels, scrubbing down one of the runs with his usual meticulous care.

"Hey, old man," Taylor called.

Cecil glanced up, his weathered face breaking into a grin. "Well, look who's hobbling around. Shouldn't you be inside?"

"I've been inside too long," she shot back. "Besides, I missed this place."

He chuckled, setting his brush aside. She saw pity cross his eyes before he hid it. "Come on, then. Let's sit a spell. You just missed Doctor Terry. She stopped by to give the puppies their next set of shots. Said they're doing just fine and will be ready to adopt out in about four weeks or so."

"Nice. I'll bet she refused payment again, too. Jaime has a heart bigger than Texas. Did you know she has her own rescue, on top of operating the busiest veterinarian practice in town?"

Cecil nodded. "Sure did. That girl is one of a kind. And she's got that alpha vibe going on. Even our most aggressive dogs don't give her any trouble."

Taylor laughed. He was right. Jaime Terry had a way of calming the biggest terrors.

They moved over to the bench near the pen of Lab puppies that had just had their second exam. They looked adorable, busy tumbling over each other to get to their mama's teats. Diesel lay at Taylor's feet, watching the puppies with mild interest. The mom thumped her tail against the dirt floor when she saw him.

"Looks like she won't mind," Taylor said. She bent over the pen and plucked a chubby pup out, sitting it in front of Diesel. The joy on his face was instant, and the pup began crawling on his head. She looked around the barn.

"Everything looks spotless in here. No thanks to me," she said. "Everyone is working more hours, and harder than they should have to because I got sick."

"You're too hard on yourself," Cecil said after a long moment of quiet.

"I just ... I hate feeling like I can't do anything," she admitted, her voice tight.

"Girl, you helped build this place with your bare hands—well, mostly bare hands. All while balancing your career and saving citizens. You and Cate have done more than most folks could dream of. You'll get back to it all in time." He gestured to Diesel. "That dog of yours knows it. Look how he sticks to you. He knows you're tougher than you think."

Taylor let out a long sigh. "Cecil, what is wrong with me? Why can't I just be enough for myself?"

He paused before answering, then looked at her with his soft brown eyes. "I don't think there's anything wrong with you. From where I stand, it's more like who you are makes total sense given what you are and where you've been."

Taylor smiled despite herself, reaching down to scratch Diesel's ears. "Maybe."

"No maybe about it," Cecil said firmly. He leaned back, watching the puppies play. "And stop rushing your recovery. You'll get there. But for now, let us handle things. Take care of yourself first. If you're so worried about getting back to this place, remember this ... We need you whole. The fully-recovered-and-determined-to-get-stuff-done-Taylor."

She didn't reply, but her heart felt lighter. Cecil always made her feel better.

Diesel nudged her hand again, and she couldn't help but laugh. He was agreeing.

"All right, all right, you two," she said, rubbing his head. "I get it. You're both Team Taylor."

"Darn right we are," Cecil said, leaning over to give her a squeeze around her shoulders. It felt so good and, for the first time in weeks, she believed it might actually be okay. But for now, she had dirty dishes and a frying pan waiting on her. A load of laundry or two. And pretty soon, a baby crying to be fed.

"C'mon, Diesel. Let's go home." Time to stop feeling sorry for herself. "Cecil, we'll catch you later."

# Chapter Twenty-Three

S hane stood in the living room of Cotton Timmons' house, the scent of mildew and stale cigarettes clinging to the air. The place was a mess—dishes piled in the sink, laundry tossed across furniture, and the floor sticky enough that Shane regretted not wearing boot covers. His eyes swept the room, searching for anything that might give them more insight into the man they were dealing with.

The last 48 hours had been a whirlwind. Someone had gone up and collected Pratt's DNA sample that morning but, bigger than that, a call had come in from the forensics lab the day before—male DNA from the Colburn house had been found, and it didn't belong to anyone in the family.

The shocker was that the match was Cotton Timmons.

Specifically, a trace amount found on the countertop of a small desk cubby in the Colburns' kitchen, right where Jane Colburn likely handled her bills and correspondence. The laptop recovered from that spot had only Jane and Willis's DNA on it, but that single trace of Timmons' DNA on the counter had been enough to secure a warrant.

Judge Crawford, who'd known Shane for years, hadn't hesitated. Within hours, Shane, Tuffin, and Hanson, along with a small forensic team, converged on Timmons' house with a full search warrant.

Now, as the others swept through the property, Shane was combing through a stack of mail on the cluttered kitchen table. He'd already found flight information to Colorado. It was jotted down on a notepad, and he'd called the airlines to confirm.

Timmons only had a one-way flight booked.

DNA found. One-way ticket to Colorado.

That pretty much told the tale, didn't it?

They needed more.

Outside, the mutt chained to a post whined pitifully. The dog had a 5-gallon bucket of cheap kibble and another of water, but how long would that last? Shane made a mental note to call animal control once this was over. If Timmons had run—and Shane's gut told him he had—then the dog needed to be turned in.

"Got some guns here," one of the GBI agents called out from the bedroom. "None match the murder weapons, though."

Shane frowned. It wasn't surprising. If Timmons was their man, he'd have been smart enough to get rid of the murder weapons by now. Still, the sheer number of firearms in his home —a couple of rifles, a shotgun, and a handgun—painted a picture of a man who liked to be prepared for ... well, something.

"Any sign of bloody clothing or towels?" Shane asked, raising his voice to carry down the hall.

"Not yet," the agent replied. "Still looking."

From the other side of the kitchen where a door led out to a laundry room\ a tech came in, holding a rag.

"Looks like blood," she said, victoriously.

Shane went to her and, with his gloved hands, took the rag. It wasn't a lot of blood. Just one corner of the rag, really.

"Bag it," he said, handing it back.

Shane continued sifting through the mail. Most of it was junk—credit card offers, past-due utility bills, and a few fishing magazines. But then something caught his eye: an open envelope from a fishing concierge company outside of Denver. The logo on the corner was a fish, its tail flicked upward as if it were mid-leap.

He pulled the folded papers out and scanned the first one quickly. A reservation for a one-day guided fishing trip, dated two days from now. Either Timmons was telling the truth, or he was damn good at setting up false leads. The invoice was marked paid from six months before. Also in the envelope was a confirmation for a hotel, booked for the next two days. But if the fishing expedition was in two days, too, was Timmons flying out immediately after he got off the boat? After a long day on the water?

That didn't make sense.

Not only that, but a one-way flight? Who does that if they plan on returning home right away? His heart thumped faster as he realized what this meant. Timmons planned to go somewhere else, likely to disappear for a while. Colorado wasn't just for a quick fishing trip—this had been premeditated. The fishing trip, if there even was one, was just the beginning.

"I think I've got something," Shane muttered to himself. He folded the papers and slid them into his pocket before standing up.

"Hey, Weaver," one of the forensic techs said, entering the room with a plastic bag in hand. Inside was a crumpled piece of paper. "Found this under the couch—county plats for both his and the Colburn property. And notes for a packing list. It mentions 'bug out gear for CO.'"

Shane nodded absently. "Good work. Keep digging." But he wasn't about to wait for them to finish. Every instinct told him

Timmons was trying to run, and Shane didn't trust anyone else to get there first.

"Weaver, you good?" Hanson asked, stepping into the kitchen, a heavy set of keys dangling from her fingers. "I found these keys and they don't fit this house or his shed."

"Great, take those over and see if any of them fit the Colburn's doors," Shane said quickly, brushing past her and heading for the door. He could feel her eyes on his back, but he didn't care. Timmons wasn't going to get away on his watch.

The sunlight was blinding as Shane stepped outside and made his way to his SUV. He climbed in, started the engine, and pulled out onto the gravel road without a word to anyone. If anyone questioned him later, he'd deal with it then. Right now, the only thing that mattered was finding Timmons before he had a chance to disappear altogether.

As Shane drove, he glanced at the fishing company's address on the paper. The small-town cop in him wasn't used to chasing suspects across state lines, but he was willing to make an exception this time. If Timmons thought he could outsmart them, he was about to learn the hard way just how wrong he was.

# Chapter Twenty-Four

Shane's boots thudded on the tiled floor of Denver International Airport as he made his way to the customer service desk and got in line behind four others. He'd had to drive all the way to Atlanta to find a flight out to Denver on such short notice, and the airport was a chaotic mess, but at least the flight itself had been uneventful. Though he knew the department wouldn't cover it, he'd splurged on business class and by his second Whiskey and Coke, and the ample room to stretch his long legs, he'd decided it was worth it.

He looked around, taking in the area around him. The design of the building was unique, unlike any other airport he'd ever been in. He hadn't seen any signs pointing to car rental, but he did see a counter for customer service. He went there and got in line. Unfortunately, they had only one clerk to serve everyone and three people were already ahead of him.

The customer being waited on stomped away, looking frustrated and Shane moved up one more. The next customer was processed quickly, and then there was only one more before his turn. Shane sighed, trying to keep his cool.

He looked at his phone and saw there were several text messages from the sheriff. Trying to bring someone in from over state lines, without getting him involved as well as the local authorities was probably going to get him in an ass load of trouble, but right now Timmons was only a suspect. Shane was going to try to nicely convince him to return to Georgia, escorted, of course. At least that was the preliminary plan, and hopefully would work out in his favor so he didn't get into too much trouble with Dawkins.

It was past dinnertime and the small meal on the plane was long ago processed, but there was no time for food right now. It was time to slip into work mode. First up, getting to the hotel Timmons was staying at.

Finally it was his turn at the counter and a young woman with a bright smile looked up at him. "Welcome to Denver International. How can I help you?"

"Hi. First time here and I have no idea where to go to pick up my car rental."

"Oh—you have to go that way," she pointed at the closest exit doors. "Look for a bus for your designated car rental company, and it'll transport you to the customer counter to pick up the keys."

"Thanks." He turned and quickly made his way to the doors and stepped outside. The views were phenomenal from the inside but, with the crisp air in his face, it really felt like Colorado now. He found the sign for Hertz and waited with a few others.

The bus came within six or seven minutes, and he sat at the front so that he could be first off. When the bus stopped, he threw a few dollar bills at the driver and hopped off, making a beeline for the counter.

"I've got a reservation," Shane said, sliding his ID and credit card across the counter. "Jeep Wrangler."

A youngish girl with a nametag that read Kayleigh tapped at the keyboard, her cheerful expression faltering. "Uh—it looks like we're out of jeeps, sir."

Shane clenched his jaw. "Out? I reserved it this morning."

"I'm really sorry," she said. "The system auto-upgraded you to another vehicle. Let me pull it up and see what we have here for you."

She turned the monitor toward him. There, in all its neon-green glory, was a compact electric car that looked more suited for a theme park than the rugged foothills of Colorado.

The guy behind him chuckled.

"You've got to be kidding me," Shane muttered, running a hand down his face.

"It's very fuel-efficient!" Kayleigh offered, her voice overly perky.

"Maybe so, but, in my book, that's not an upgrade. I wouldn't be caught dead in an electric car. Do you have anything else? A truck? An SUV? Anything not electric?"

Kayleigh shook her head sadly. "I'm sorry but we're completely booked up."

Shane glared at her but bit back a retort. He didn't know how they could not give him what he reserved, but what was he going to do? Arrest her?

"Fine. Just give me the keys."

Moments later, he was squeezing himself into the tiny car, its cheery beep mocking him as he settled into the seat. The steering wheel felt like a toy in his hands, and he grumbled under his breath as he pulled up the hotel address on his phone GPS, then pulled out of the lot.

Denver's skyline stretched behind him in the moonlight, the peaks of the Rockies rising like a wall of indifference.

The forty-five-minute drive crawled along in after-dinner

traffic. By the time he pulled up in front of the Hampton Inn & Suites hotel, his patience was shot.

Inside the hotel lobby, the air was cool and smelled faintly of lavender. A young desk clerk greeted him with a polite smile.

"Hi there! Checking in?"

"Not quite," Shane replied, pulling out his badge. "I'm Detective Weaver, coming in from Georgia and I'm looking for a guest. Cotton Timmons. Can you tell me which room he's in?"

The clerk's smile faltered. "I'm sorry, sir. We can't give out that kind of information. It's company policy put in place for our guests' safety."

Shane sighed, leaning in slightly. "Listen, this is official business, and I need to find him."

The clerk shifted uncomfortably. "I'll get my manager."

Before Shane could respond, the manager emerged from an office behind the desk. She was tall, with dark hair swept into a sleek ponytail, and her navy-blue blazer couldn't hide the confident way she carried herself. Her name tag read Jillian.

"Is there a problem?" she asked, her voice smooth and professional.

Shane explained the situation, flashing his badge again. Jillian listened intently, her dark eyes sharp as she processed his words.

"Let me check," she said finally, moving to the computer. Her fingers danced across the keyboard before she straightened and turned back to him. "It looks like Mr. Timmons never checked in."

Shane frowned. "Are you sure? I know for sure that he had a reservation."

"I'm certain," Jillian said. "We're the only hotel with this name in the area."

Shane exhaled sharply, frustration bubbling under the

surface. "Alright. Any chance you've got a room available for tonight?"

Jillian's lips curved into a slight smile. "We do. Let me get you set up."

Within minutes, she handed him a key card, but, instead of pulling away, she slid a small piece of paper across the counter. Shane glanced at it. Scrawled in neat handwriting was a phone number.

She leaned in slightly, her voice just low enough for only him to hear. She wore a light scent that tickled his sense. Something floral. "If you want to grab a nightcap later, I'm off at ten."

For a moment, Shane stared at her, caught off guard. He nodded faintly, slipping the paper into his pocket without a word.

Up in his room, he dropped his bag by the door and pulled out his laptop, settling onto the bed. He skimmed his emails, hoping for updates, but none were important enough to reply to. He opened up a document and began jotting notes.

*Timmons reserved hotel room at Hampton Inn*
*Reserved fishing trip with Fly Guys*
*Didn't check in to hotel—did he leave the reservation at Hampton Inn to throw them off?*
*Will he show for fishing guide?*

What he needed to do was to start calling all the hotels in Denver to see if Cotton had checked in. Shit—they weren't going to give him that information over the phone. He'd have to show his badge in person. That was definitely a snag.

He considered his options.

The most logical thing to do was to show up for the same fishing expedition in the morning and grab him there.

He picked up his phone and seeing a handful of missed calls from Mira, he dialed her number. She picked up on the first ring, her tone already exasperated.

"Shane," she said, sighing heavily. "Where the hell are you?"

"I'm sorry I missed your calls and texts," Shane said, though the words felt hollow. "I was in the air and now I'm in Denver."

"Denver? In Colorado?" she asked, her tone incredulous.

"Yeah. Sorry," he said, running his hand through his thick hair. She was pissed. And rightfully so. "It's for work and I didn't have any notice. This investigation is complicated, Mira. There's a lot going on that I can't share with you."

"That's always your excuse," Mira snapped. "You could've called me on the way to the airport. Or shot me a text. Why don't you just admit it? You never have time for me or for this relationship. Shane, I can't keep doing this."

He pinched the bridge of his nose. "I understand. You're right, you deserve better than what I can give you."

There was a long pause on the line. "You're not even going to fight for this, are you?"

"Mira ..." Shane trailed off. He couldn't muster the energy to argue.

"Goodbye, Shane," she said, her voice tight, before the line went dead.

He set the phone on the nightstand and leaned back against the pillows. The breakup felt inevitable, and, to his surprise, it didn't hurt as much as he thought it would. He was relieved.

Soon, his thoughts drifted to Taylor. Weeks of silence stretched between them, and though he told himself she needed to focus on her health, so she could get back to work, her absence gnawed at him.

His phone buzzed with texts—updates from the sheriff and

Tuffin—but Shane ignored them. Until Timmons was in custody, he didn't trust anyone not to spook the man.

With a sigh, he kicked off his boots and stretched out on the bed, still fully clothed. He'd just close his eyes for a minute. Then he'd get up and go find something to eat. Maybe even have that nightcap with—

Sleep claimed him before he could even finish the thought.

# Chapter Twenty-Five

B right and early the next morning, Shane sat at a picnic
table outside the South Platte River marina, the
morning air crisp and thick with the faint scent of pine
and wet earth. The marina was tucked just outside Denver, near
the Four Corners region, where the mountains loomed in the
distance. The rhythmic clink of fishing equipment filled the air
as two men from Fly Guys Fishing Guides worked around their
boat, loading rods, reels, waders, and other gear.

He was cold as hell and Shane took a sip of his coffee,
watching the scene unfold from behind a pair of dark
sunglasses. He'd arrived at dawn, scoping out the location and
keeping an eye out for Cotton Timmons. The dock was busy
but not chaotic, and the Fly Guys boat stood out with its logo
emblazoned on the side in bold, orange letters.

It was only about a fifty-fifty chance in Shane's mind that
Timmons would make an appearance. More than likely, he was
already on the run, hundreds or thousands of miles away from
Colorado, which he'd used as a diversion. Still yet, it had to be
checked out.

Fifteen minutes before the appointed time, Shane spotted

an old Ford pickup truck pulling into the gravel lot. Much to his relief, Timmons hopped out of the passenger seat, flanked by two men who looked like they hadn't worried about a thing in their lives. They were laughing, hauling a cooler out of the truck bed along with a couple of fishing rods and tackle boxes. They headed for the dock.

Shane set his coffee down and rose from his bench, keeping his pace deliberate as he intercepted them before they could reach the boat.

"Cotton Timmons," Shane called, his voice firm.

Timmons froze, his laughter dying instantly. His face twisted into a mixture of shock and anger. "What the hell are you doing here?"

The two men with him exchanged confused glances. "Who's this?" one of them asked.

"Shane Weaver, Detective," Shane said, flashing his badge. He turned his gaze back to Timmons. "We need to talk."

Timmons shook his head, his hands balling into fists. "No way. I've got a fishing trip, man. I done told you everything you wanted to know, and you can't just show up here and ruin my trip!"

The two Fly Guys employees on the boat looked up, concern flashing across their faces. One of them, a grizzled man in his forties who looked like he'd seen his share of drama on these waters, climbed onto the dock and approached.

"I'm Will, and I'm in charge of this charter. What's going on here?"

"This guy's harassing me," Timmons snapped, gesturing toward Shane.

Shane held up his badge again. "I'm not harassing anyone. This is official business."

The foreman's eyes narrowed as he looked between Timmons and Shane. "I can vouch for these guys. They come every year but, if there's a problem, I'm not taking anyone out on my boat until it's cleared up. Last thing I need is my company wrapped up in something illegal."

Timmons turned to his friends, his face reddening. "Can you believe this?"

One of his friends clapped him on the shoulder. "Look, Cotton. Just go talk to him and get it over with. We want to fish, man."

Timmons grumbled under his breath but finally nodded.

Shane gestured toward a picnic table near the parking lot, keeping a close eye on Timmons as they walked. Every muscle in Shane's body was coiled, ready in case Timmons tried to make a run for it. He didn't look like he could outrun a toddler, but you never knew.

When they reached the table, he stood close enough to ensure Timmons couldn't bolt.

"Let's go over this again," Shane began, his tone sharp. "First, let me ask you, why did you make a reservation at the Hampton Inn but never check in?"

Timmons gestured toward the dock, where his friends were waiting impatiently. "Because they picked me up at the airport. We went back to Max's place for a cookout and beer. I drank too much, so Max insisted I stay in his guest room. Is that a crime?"

Shane's eyes narrowed. "This is all convenient timing, don't you think? A fishing trip just as we're narrowing in on you as a suspect."

Timmons threw his hands in the air. "I've had this trip planned for a year! Ask my buddies if you don't believe me. What the hell is your problem?"

"My problem," Shane said, his voice lowering, "is that, even if you did have this trip planned for a year, maybe you planned the murders to coincide, so you'd have a reason to leave town. I just got word that your DNA was found in the Colburns' house. So let me ask you again—have you ever been inside?"

Timmons' face turned crimson. "I've told you a hundred times—I've never been in that house!"

"Then how do you explain your DNA being there?"

Timmons' voice rose in frustration. "I can't! If my DNA is in that house, someone planted it there. I don't know how, but I wasn't there, and I wasn't part of that crime!"

Shane studied him, his instincts screaming that something wasn't adding up. "If you're innocent," he said, his tone softening just slightly, "then you need to come back with me and prove it."

Timmons looked over at his friends near the boat, then glared at Shane, his jaw tightening. "And if I say no? What are my options?"

Shane was nervous. He couldn't legally detain Timmons.

He had to decide if he was going to do it anyway. But first he'd try persuasion and bending the truth. He leaned in like he was telling him a secret and changed his tone to a friendly one. Now it was time to play the buddy role.

"Listen, Timmons. As you know, the state GBI is now on this case. It's a big deal and, unless you want to spend the rest of your life on the run with the photo from your driver's license flashed on every news channel from coast to coast, I suggest you come back with me and straighten this mess out. I can help you."

For a moment, they stood there, locked in a silent battle of wills. Finally, Timmons let out a heavy sigh. "Fine," he said, his voice dripping with resignation. "But you better believe I'll be calling my lawyer the second we get to the airport."

Shane nodded. "That's your right."

He placed a firm hand on Timmons' shoulder, guiding him

back toward the parking lot. His eyes scanned the marina one last time, ensuring no surprises were waiting for them.

"Guys, go on without me," Timmons yelled out to his friends, throwing his arms in the air in a frustrated and overly dramatic gesture.

As they walked, Shane's mind churned with questions. Timmons' story had holes big enough to drive a truck through, but the man's indignation felt genuine. One way or another, Shane was determined to get to the truth—no matter how tangled the line.

# Chapter Twenty-Six

Taylor eased into the worn leather chair in her sunlit living room, holding a steaming cup of herbal tea and a book about moving on from trauma that her therapist had recommended.

*"Pay attention to your patterns. The way you learned to survive may not be the way you want to continue to live your life."* Such a great quote and one that felt pertinent not only to her own life, but to her sisters and her mother.

Lennon sat only a foot or so away in her bouncy seat, cooing quietly as she played with the new selection of toys Sam had hung in front of it the night before.

"You will never have to heal from your childhood," Taylor whispered to her, meaning it from the bottom of her heart.

She sipped from her mug, savoring the faint taste of Chai. From Alice's room, she could hear the faint sounds of Quig laughing with Alice. They were doing homework, and turns out that Quig was a math geek, the only subject that Alice needed help with at times.

Taylor still couldn't quite believe it. A few weeks ago, the thought of hiring an assistant/nanny—especially someone she'd met in jail—would've seemed absurd. But in just over a week and a half, Quig had turned out to be nothing short of a miracle.

The idea had been Sam's, of all people. After another tense morning where Taylor had been trying to juggle Lennon, Johnny, laundry, and a pile of paperwork, he'd suggested it.

Since Lucy had gone to stay at Jo's house and left Johnny with them, Taylor had even more to come home to worry about. They felt Johnny was best with them, so they didn't want to say anything to Lucy about helping, but it was a lot.

"What about Quig?" he'd said, as casually as if he were suggesting takeout for dinner.

"Quig?" Taylor had blinked at him in disbelief. "From jail? Are you serious?"

Sam had shrugged. "You need someone you are really comfortable with, and she's got a good heart. You said so your-self. She's obviously eager to turn her life around. And it's not like we're hiring her to manage finances or to be a nanny. I heard her tell you how hard it is to get a good job since she has a crim-inal background. She could help you around here."

"Sam, I really like Quig and, yes, we bonded, but we can't let someone we don't know that well handle our baby," she'd said.

"That's fine. There's still housework, cooking, and errands. And once we trust her completely, we can consider letting her help with Lennon. You've got enough going on without trying to do it all alone, and you refuse to rest like you should when I'm outside working. You also feel guilty that you aren't helping on the farm, and, if we had someone to help, I could step in more and you could relax."

"Sam, don't be ridiculous," Taylor said. "I'm fine. Really—I am."

But that night, she'd thought about how much help Quig could be, and how the girl was stuck working a job she hated, because of her past mistakes. The next day, they made the call. Quig had shown up on her doorstep within hours, a duffel bag slung over her shoulder, her wide grin betraying both nerves and excitement. Considering it was far from a glamorous or high-paying job they were offering; Quig was pretty excited.

"I promise, I won't let you down," she'd said earnestly, her fingers twisting the strap of her bag.

And so far, she hadn't. In just a short time, Quig had seamlessly integrated into their lives. She had a knack for reading the room, knowing exactly when to step in and when to hang back. In the mornings, Quig was there at six and, while Taylor nursed and took care of Lennon, Quig balanced the chaos of bottles, toys, and a perpetually sticky highchair. Whether it be a dirty sink or a pile of laundry, when she saw something that needed done, she dived into it without being asked.

By late afternoon when Lennon was down for a nap, Quig was in the barn, tending to the animals or checking in with boarders. She was efficient in the kennels, and the animals loved her. Cecil swore she was a pale angel sent from heaven to keep him entertained with all her stories. Turns out she'd led quite a colorful life thus far.

Taken to her instantly, Cecil welcomed Quig into his cabin like a long-lost daughter. On the nights he needed to stay on the farm, he slept on the couch in the office, but Sam said that he'd seen Cecil and Quig in the evenings on his porch, swapping stories and sipping sweet tea next to a small heater.

Quig tried to tell him that she didn't mind him sleeping under the same roof, but he claimed he didn't want to sully a young woman's reputation, ignoring the fact that Quig was a felon who had three children by three different men. He pretended not to see the teardrop tattoo next to her eye, and the scar from over her eyebrow where she'd had another one removed.

175

Despite her background, everyone liked Quig. It was a good lesson for the younger kids that they should never judge anyone based on appearance. Quig sure didn't look like the girl next door, and she had a record to boot, but, in her core, she was a genuinely nice person who only wanted to help everyone. The fact that she'd made a lot of bad decisions in her life was something they didn't talk about.

Even Alice was over the moon because, now that Quig was around, there were less chores and more reading time for her, though she'd never complained much about helping out.

Taylor couldn't deny the shift in the house's energy. Now that things were running smoother and getting done, there was less tension. For Taylor specifically there was less of the overwhelming pressure that had been crushing her for months.

But as much as Taylor appreciated Quig's presence, there was still a part of her that struggled to let go of her many responsibilities. Worries, too. Like about Lucy, who didn't seem to be improving as fast as she should.

Also about her helping out with the family business. Sam was stepping up more, but Taylor felt guilty that her position had been taken apart, her responsibilities doled out to Cate and her sisters—with Ellis, Sam, and Cecil—and now Quig, too, to take up her slack.

"Taylor?"

Quig's voice pulled her from her thoughts. She approached from the hallway. "Want me to keep Lennon company while you catch a break. Maybe take a nap? I still have an hour before I'm due at the barn."

Taylor hesitated, her fingers tightening around her mug. "You don't have to do that. You've already been running around all morning. Why don't you rest?"

Quig grinned, her eyes sparkling. "Nah, napping is hard for me. Too much nervous energy. Alice is done with her homework, and my other choice is going down early to help Jo with the goat pen. Honestly, Lennon is way more fun than goat poop, but I am fine with either task."

Taylor laughed despite herself. "Alright. But I'm not going to nap. I think I'll walk down and talk to Jo for a bit. Get some fresh air. If Lennon gets fussy, text me."

"Will do, but don't forget to stand upwind from the goats if you want fresh air." She laughed as she plopped down and took a place on the floor in front of Lennon, who smiled widely and kicked her feet, happy at the sight of her new friend.

Taylor slid her feet into her muck boots, grabbed a coat, and stepped outside. The quick slap of crisp air stung her cheeks but was a relief from the too warm interior of the house. Sam insisted they keep the temperature at seventy-three degrees for Lennon, and sometimes it felt like a sauna.

She looked back through the window of the door one more time before stepping off the porch. It was still strange, this feeling of not being entirely needed. For so long, she'd been the one holding everything together, the glue that kept her family from crumbling. But now, with Quig's help and Sam's encouragement, Taylor was starting to realize that maybe she didn't have to carry the weight alone. She'd also been making strides with putting thoughts of her job aside and hadn't contacted Shane since she'd arrived home.

She did wonder about the Colburn case, but the realization that she really could step away from it did wonders for her mental state. The thought of having that freedom was both liberating and terrifying. It presented so many questions.

Who was she without being a deputy and protecting the town?

What was she supposed to do with her dream of making detective one day?

Could being a wife and mother, and sharing duties with the family business, be enough?

A few buzzards circled over her head in the clear, blue sky, reminding her that not everything was rosy. Right now, things were good but, somewhere, something troublesome was always brewing.

# Chapter Twenty-Seven

The sharp crunch of her boots against frozen earth filled the air as Taylor trudged toward the barn. Her breath came in visible puffs, mingling with the crisp scent of hay and animal musk. She stopped at the goat pen and leaned against the wooden gate, taking in the scene. Jo, clad in her pink flamingo muck boots, men's Carhartt pants and a flannel shirt, was knee-deep in the goat pen, wielding a shovel like a knight with a sword.

"Hey, Jo," Taylor called, resting her forearms on the fence.

Jo glanced up, brushing a strand of hair from her face with the back of her hand. "Hey, Tay. What're you doing all the way out here?"

Taylor smiled faintly. "Needed some fresh air. Want some help with that?"

Jo scoffed, waving her off with the shovel. "Help? You? The new mom who can barely stay awake past eight? Nah, I've got this."

"Jo," Taylor protested, stepping closer. "Come on, I can muck a pen. I used to do it all the time before life got crazy."

Jo planted the pitchfork in the straw with a decisive thud. "Taylor, I'd love your company, but you're not picking up a shovel and, before you ask, you aren't putting down hay, either. Just sit there and supervise."

Taylor sighed but relented, perching on the edge of the fence. One of the goats, a mischievous-looking doe with a patchy brown coat, sauntered up to her and bleated loudly in her face.

"Well, hello to you, too," Taylor said, gently nudging the goat's nose.

"That's Dandelion," Jo said with a smirk. "She's got a crush on Quig. Follows her everywhere because, right now, she's the biggest Houdini of Walsh Wild Hearts Rescue. Always getting out of the pen and we haven't figured it out yet."

Taylor laughed, picturing Quig trying to fend off the goat's affections. "I can only imagine how Quig deals with that."

"Oh, it's a riot," Jo said, grinning. "Yesterday, she was trying to feed the chickens, and Dandelion kept sticking her nose in the feed bucket. Quig finally gave up and tried to distract her with a handful of alfalfa, but Dandelion wasn't having it. Ended up knocking the bucket over and scattering feed everywhere. The chickens had a field day."

Taylor shook her head, chuckling. "Quig and Dandelion. Sounds like a comedy duo."

"Yeah, it's good to have some laughter around here," Jo said, her tone softening. She leaned on her pitchfork, studying Taylor. "How are you holding up, really?"

Taylor hesitated, kicking at the dirt with the toe of her boot. "Better. It helps having Quig around. And Sam's been great. But ... I can't stop worrying about Lucy. She really worried me the way she was acting at my house. Anything changed?"

Jo sighed, tossing a pile of soiled straw into a wheelbarrow. "Nah, she's the same at my place. Now she's spending hours doing her hair, blasting music, and making a mess of Levi's room. He didn't mind giving it up at first, but now he's getting salty. Says it looks like a tornado hit it every day."

Taylor winced. "I hate that she's putting you through all this. You've got enough on your plate."

"Don't start," Jo said firmly, warding off any talk of her own personal struggles. "She's a great distraction. And I don't worry as much as you do because, let's be honest, this isn't new. Lucy's been wreaking havoc since we were kids. Remember when she convinced everyone in junior high that the Principal Clark was running some secret conspiracy? She had the whole school in an uproar."

Taylor laughed despite herself. "Oh my gosh, I forgot about that. And didn't she glue all the classroom locks shut one night to 'prove her theory'? Dad was so mad when he got called up there."

That was a memory they'd never forget. He'd dragged all of them with him and they'd been embarrassed because he smelled like a brewery, but she didn't mention that part.

Jo nodded, her smile fading. "See? She's always been this way—paranoid, rebellious. I used to think it was just teenage drama, but now … I wonder if it's something more. Like, maybe she's had this … *thing* brewing in her head all along, and it's just gotten worse over time."

Taylor's expression sobered. What she meant by *thing* was mental illness. It was still hard for them to speak the words. "I always thought it was the trauma of losing Mom so young. Like she was acting out because she didn't know how to process it. But … maybe you're right. Maybe it's something deeper."

Jo shrugged, her gaze distant as she moved to the bales of straw. "Who knows? I just hope we can figure it out before it's too late."

"The fact that she's going longer and longer without spending time with Johnny is especially concerning. He's starting to not ask about her as much, too."

They fell into a contemplative silence, broken only by the rustle of straw and the occasional bleat from the goats.

Finally, Jo straightened and stretched, her hands resting on her hips. "Speaking of figuring things out," she said, glancing at Taylor. "I know I'm not supposed to ask but I'm dying to know. Any updates on the Colburn case? Heard anything from Shane?"

Taylor shook her head quickly. "Nope. Haven't talked to him. Swear."

Jo raised an eyebrow, clearly unconvinced. "Uh-huh. Sure, Taylor."

"I'm serious," Taylor insisted. "I've been staying out of it. Trying to focus on the kids and getting better."

Jo sighed, propping the pitchfork against the fence. "I keep thinking about the two daughters. It's all so tragic, though. Losing both parents and their brother in one night? And now Seth and Erin's kids ... They're sure gonna have to grow up leaning on each other. Makes me think of us. How we've always had to stick together. Well, at least when one of us wasn't battling with another. I'll admit, sometimes we were at war but look at us now; we made it without killing each other. So far—knock on wood." She thumped her knuckle against the fence post.

Something about Jo's words sparked a thought in Taylor's mind. Her brow furrowed as a memory surfaced, something she'd come across while digging into Seth Colburn's background before she went on leave.

"I need to get back to the house," Taylor said abruptly, hopping off the fence.

Jo frowned. "What is it?"

"Just remembered something," Taylor said vaguely, already heading toward the barn door. "I'll tell you later."

Jo called after her, but Taylor didn't stop. Her heart raced as she made her way back to the house, her mind spinning with possibilities. If what she suspected was true, it could change everything.

# Chapter Twenty-Eight

Shane stared at his laptop, the subject line from Taylor's email catching his eye like a flashing neon sign in the dark. "We need to talk—urgent." He clicked it, his pulse quickening as he scanned the lines. The bombshell hit him hard, but, before he could process it fully, Dawkins' voice echoed in his mind: he and Tuffin were to question Cotton Timmons together. And now, Timmons' lawyer was in the mix, already making things difficult before the interview even began.

Tamping down his emotions, Shane grabbed his phone and dialed Deputy Kuno. "I need you to find Missy Ann Colburn. Right now. Pick her up quietly and bring her in. Don't spook her. Got it?"

Kuno hesitated for only a moment before replying, "Doesn't she live up near Atlanta?

"Yep. Which means you need to get on the road now."

"On it."

Shane hung up, pushed Taylor's email out of his mind, and walked into the conference room where the attorney, a wiry man with sharp features named Gerald Reese, was already seated next to Timmons. Reese was flipping through a stack of papers with a bored expression, but Shane knew better than to underestimate him. He was one of those defense lawyers who thrived on theatrics, always one step ahead of the prosecution.

Tuffin gave Shane an irritated look.

"Detective Weaver," Reese said without looking up. "Before we begin, let's set some ground rules. My client will not answer repetitive questions, nor will he tolerate harassment. You ask a question; you get one clear response. Anything beyond that, and this is over. Understood?"

Shane exchanged a glance with Tuffin, who shrugged. "Let's get on with it," Shane said curtly, dropping into a chair across from them.

Tuffin opened with polite, measured questions about Timmons' recent travel, his property, and his relationships with the Colburns. Reese sat silent, his eyes darting between Tuffin and his client, but it was clear he wasn't overly concerned.

Then Shane leaned forward, his voice sharp. "Let's talk about those property plats we found at your place, Cotton. Why were you mapping out the Colburn property?"

Timmons' smirk faltered. "I wasn't. I was checking my fence line. Their damn dog kept getting into my yard, tearing up my garden. You've heard about that, haven't you?" He leaned back in his chair, crossing his arms.

"Maybe you should be more concerned with your own dog, the way you care—or should I say don't care—for him, Mr. Timmons," Shane said sarcastically.

Reese held up a hand. "Careful with the tone, Detective. My client has answered your question."

Shane ignored him and pulled out a photo of the bloody rag they'd recovered. "Explain this."

Timmons rolled his eyes. "I hit my thumb with a hammer putting up chicken wire. You want to process it? Go ahead. It's my blood, and you'll find chicken crap on it, too."

Reese tilted his head and gave Shane a mock-sympathetic smile. "Shame your department's wasting resources on this nonsense, Detective."

Shane didn't give him the satisfaction of a reaction. Instead, he pulled out another item: the packing list titled "Bug Out List."

Timmons snorted. "I always call it that. It's just my way of saying I'm getting out of town. You're reaching, Detective."

"Why the one-way flight to Colorado, then?" Shane pressed.

Timmons shrugged, looking genuinely exasperated. "Because it's cheaper to book a one-way last minute, and I can grab a red-eye home when I'm done. What's the big deal?"

Shane leaned closer, lowering his voice. "The big deal is how your DNA ended up in the Colburns' house. You're telling me you've never been inside, yet there it is, tying you to the scene. You want to explain that?"

Timmons' face darkened, his fists clenching. "I've already told you—I've never been in their damn house. If my DNA's there, someone planted it. I didn't kill them."

Reese placed a firm hand on Timmons' arm, a silent signal to rein in his anger. "Detective, you're attempting to paint my client as a murderer with no evidence beyond speculation. We'll entertain a few more questions, but tread carefully."

Shane pushed further, walking Timmons through the timeline of the murders. "First, you get into the house, maybe through a back door. Then you corner the Colburns, and things escalate. You grab a weapon—"

"Enough!" Timmons slammed his fists on the table, his face red. "That's a damn lie, and you know it!"

"Oh, is it, though?" Shane said. "Let's talk about how you caught felony charges for abuse on your wife and kids. Don't tell me you don't have the capacity for violence, Timmons. It's in the records, black and white."

Before Shane could press harder, Reese stood abruptly, cutting in sharply. "We're done here. This has gone far enough. My client will not be subjected to your baseless accusations any longer. No more questions for today."

The room was tense as Reese guided Timmons out. Timmons threw a glare over his shoulder at Shane, muttering, "This isn't over."

"Good job, Weaver. Now he's gone," Tuffin said, banging his notebook shut. He got up and slammed out the door.

Shane sat back, his jaw tight with frustration. They didn't have enough—a shaky case wouldn't hold in court, and, until they got more, they couldn't risk it.

Letting Timmons go felt like losing, and Shane hated it. He walked out of the room, his mind churning with doubts and anger. The one thing he knew for certain was that this wasn't over—not by a long shot.

* * *

Shane closed the door to the small interview room, coffee in one hand and a notepad in the other. Missy Ann Colburn sat across the table, her hands folded tightly in her lap. Her face betrayed nothing but mild irritation, though Shane knew better than to trust outward appearances.

Thankfully she hadn't lawyered up.

He slid the coffee across the table to her. "Cream and sugar, just like you asked. Thanks for meeting with me, Missy Ann."

"Yeah, sure," she muttered, wrapping her hands around the cup.

Shane took a seat, leaning back casually, but his eyes stayed locked on hers. He read her rights to her before he began. "Let's start simple. Tell me about your childhood. What was it like growing up in your house?"

Missy Ann's expression softened, and she gave a small, reminiscent smile. "It was good, you know? Simple. We didn't have a lot of frivolous things, but we had enough. They were good parents, really. Supportive. They let us figure things out on our own, mostly."

"Mostly?" Shane pressed.

She laughed softly. "Yeah, I mean, we didn't get punished much. They weren't the overly strict type. Except for Seth. Dad was harder on him. Sometimes ... he'd use the belt."

Shane raised an eyebrow, jotting that down. "Why Seth? Was he a troublemaker?"

Missy Ann shrugged. "He just ... acted out more than we did. When he got into his teenage years, he pushed limits. Maybe because he was the only boy and felt like he had something to prove. I don't know."

Shane nodded, switching gears. "What about your little sister, Raya? What was she like growing up?"

Missy Ann scoffed, her smile fading. "She got away with everything. Always the baby of the family, you know?"

"She didn't get into trouble?"

"No, not really, other than always being moody. She did well in school, but not good enough for any scholarships. My parents would've helped her with college, but Raya didn't want to go. Didn't want to leave home or this town, but Mom convinced her to finally get the apartment, thinking it would help her grow up. Later ... well, she couldn't hack it financially. So Mom and Dad bought her that mobile home, set it up for her rent-free. She's been living there ever since."

"How'd that make you feel?" Shane asked, watching her reaction closely.

Missy Ann hesitated, her fingers tightening around the

coffee cup. "I mean, yeah, I didn't feel great about it when they told me. Not angry, exactly, but ... frustrated. Mom and Dad had helped Seth, too. With the down payment on his house. But I never took anything from them. I did it on my own. I did tell Mom it was time to think about themselves for once and stop bailing people out. She said she was going to tell Raya and Ronnie they had to start paying rent."

"Did they ever have that conversation?"

Missy Ann sighed. "Yes. She told them."

"Did they begin paying?"

"I don't know. I never brought it up again."

"Hmm ..." Shane said. "I bet it was hard to watch your sister always being babied and getting things she didn't work for. Then not even to act grateful for it. That had to stick in your craw."

"What is that supposed to mean?" she asked.

"Nothing." Shane scribbled a note, then looked back up. "Has Raya ever been violent? Or has she been diagnosed with any sort of mental illness?"

Missy Ann's head snapped up, her eyes narrowing. "No. Why are you asking me stuff like this? You're not thinking my sister and I had anything to do with this, are you?"

Shane held up a hand, his tone calm. "I'm not thinking anything. Just gathering information."

Missy Ann crossed her arms, clearly on the defensive now. "I mean—you are way off the trail if you suspect me. And as for Raya, she's always been a pain in the butt and, yeah, sometimes she was mad at all of us, but not for a minute do I think she'd ever be capable of annihilating her own family."

Shane decided to give her a pause.

"Excuse me for just a second." Without waiting for a response, he stepped out into the hallway, texting Deputy Kuno.

"Bring Raya and Ronnie in ASAP. Quietly. Don't give them a heads-up before you pick them up."

When he slipped back into the room, Missy Ann was texting. She put the phone down quickly.

"Okay, Missy Ann. Let's talk about your ex-husband."

"Tommy? Why him?"

"Well, he was once a part of your family, and you have a child together. How contentious was the divorce?"

"Not at all. It was amicable, and we have no issues with each other. We just couldn't be a couple. We co-parent our son just fine, though."

"How did he get along with your parents? Your siblings?"

"Great," she said. "Listen, Tommy is a lot of things but he's not violent. He always got along with my family, and I didn't poison them against him when we split up. As a matter of fact, Tommy gave Seth his first job in construction, and, when my brother went off on his own, Tommy walked him through getting his contractor's license. As far as I know, they were still friends. Until ... until—"

Her eyes watered.

"Yeah, I get it," Shane said, rescuing her from the terrible words. "Until the incidents. What about Seth and Raya? Were they close?"

She nodded, but she still looked on guard. "Yeah, all through primary school they were like two peas in a pod. But when Seth met Erin and started dating her, things changed. He kind of went his own way."

"Was Raya jealous?"

Missy Ann shrugged again. "Maybe a little. I don't know. She never said anything to me about it. She's not the type to voice her issues. She'd rather sit and stew about it."

Shane leaned forward slightly. "Did Raya and Seth ever have a business together?"

Missy Ann frowned, shaking her head at first, but then paused. "Oh, wait. Yeah, they did. An auto body shop, years ago. I can't even remember when. I know that Seth's construction business hadn't taken off yet, and his credit wasn't great. He talked Raya into taking out a loan to get it started. They signed a lease for a shop, got signage and, at first, things were good."

"What happened?"

"Didn't last two months," Missy Ann said, her voice laced with disdain. "Raya wouldn't do her part—couldn't keep the customers lined up or handle the books. Seth gave up trying to juggle everything himself, so they shut it down."

"And the loan?"

Missy Ann shrugged. "Far as I know, no one paid it off. But I do know Raya's been going on for months about how Seth owes her money. Something about wanting to pay off some old debt. Maybe it's tied to that. Who knows?"

"Was Raya having financial trouble?"

"Probably. She's terrible with money," Missy Ann said, her tone bitter.

"And Ronnie? When did he come into the picture?"

"Not long ago. He moved into the apartment with her but, according to Mama, he wasn't much help paying the bills. That's part of why they bought the mobile home."

Shane nodded, filing that away. "What about Ronnie and Seth? Did they get along?"

Missy Ann hesitated. "I guess. Ronnie's quiet—doesn't say much. Everyone gets along with him because, well, he doesn't really give you a reason not to. Raya does all the talking for them."

"And your dad? Did he like Ronnie?"

She pursed her lips. "Hard to tell. Dad was the type to keep his thoughts to himself. But I know he tried to bring Ronnie out of his shell—make him feel like he was welcome into our family.

He took him fishing once, even had him help with some remodeling in the kitchen. Far as I know, it went fine."

"Did he pay him for his help?"

"I'm sure he did. Dad wouldn't have expected him to work for free. But I don't know for sure."

Shane took another note before his next question. He looked up, wanting to see her reaction on this one. "Do you know if Raya or Ronnie own weapons?"

Missy Ann's eyes widened, and she shifted uncomfortably. "No ... not that I know of. But you're starting to scare me with some of your questions, Detective Weaver."

"Nothing to be scared of," Shane said smoothly. "Just doing my job." He paused, then asked, "Would you mind if I take a look at your phone?"

Missy Ann faltered, clearly taken aback. "I mean, if you really need to. I don't have anything to hide," she said after a moment, sliding it across the table and telling him her passcode.

"Thanks," Shane said, standing up. "I'm going to hang onto this for a bit. Sheriff might have a few more questions for you. Sit tight, okay? I'll have someone bring you some lunch."

# Chapter Twenty-Nine

Shane went directly from the interview room to the sheriff's office and knocked on the door before easing it open. Dawkins looked up a scowl already on his face.

"Got a minute?" Shane asked.

"Depends," Dawkins replied, setting his pen aside. "Have you figured out why you're spending so much valuable time chasing after the Colburn sisters when Timmons was your prime suspect as of this morning?"

Shane stepped inside, closing the door behind him. "He might still be. But there are gaps in the Colburns' stories that I need to close. Missy Ann left me with more questions than answers, and now I need to talk to Raya. Ronnie, too."

The sheriff leaned back in his chair, crossing his arms. "You think the sisters are involved?"

"I didn't say that. At this point, I think they know more than they're letting on. And if we don't follow this thread, we might miss something important."

Dawkins studied him for a long moment before sighing. "Fine. But don't lose sight of Timmons. He's still the one with motive, proximity, and opportunity."

Shane nodded, stepping out before the sheriff could change his mind.

In the interview room, Raya sat with her arms crossed tightly over her chest. She looked like hell, her stringy brown hair hanging in her pale face. Of course she would—her parents who she depended on were swept away from her in an instant.

When she heard him enter, she lifted her head, and her carefully neutral expression faltered as Shane entered and slid into the seat across from her.

"Thanks for coming in, Raya," he said, his tone casual. "I've got a few follow-up questions. Just want to clarify some things. So you know, everything we do or say in this room is being recorded. Do you mind if I read you your rights?"

"You did that the other day."

"I know I did, but I like to just play by policy every time. It's just procedure."

"Sure," she said flatly.

Shane read her rights, then started with easy questions, guiding her through her upbringing and family dynamics. Her answers were polite but clipped, until he brought up Missy Ann.

"She mentioned you two didn't always see eye to eye," Shane said.

Raya let out a short, bitter laugh. "Oh really? That's what she said? Well, she's always had it easy. The nice house, the divorce settlement that set her up for life. Meanwhile, I've had to scrape by."

"But Missy Ann went to college, right? Built a career?"

"Yeah, well, school wasn't for me," Raya said, her tone sharp. "It was just a place for more people to judge me. I wouldn't fit in like she did."

Shane nodded, his expression sympathetic. "I hear you on

that. I wasn't college material, either. And what about Seth? You two were close once, weren't you?"

Raya's face softened slightly. "Yeah. We used to be. He'd help me with my car, stuff like that. But after he got with Erin, everything changed. It was like I didn't exist anymore."

A knock on the door interrupted the next question on the tip of Shane's tongue.

"Excuse me," he said, getting up. He opened the door and stepped into the hallway.

"Weaver, we have something new." Sheriff Dawkins said. "Timmons came back with his lawyer and gave another sworn statement. It's about how his DNA could've gotten into the crime scene."

He handed the paper over to Shane, who read it and nodded.

"I thought as much," he said, handing it back.

"Get back in there and don't come out until you have something," Dawkins said.

Shane nodded. "Will do."

When he returned to the room, Raya was sitting still, scrolling through her phone.

"Okay, where were we," he said, his tone shifting to casual curiosity. "Oh, about Seth. Did the two of you ever go into business together?"

Raya stiffened, avoiding his gaze. "Why does that matter?"

"Just trying to understand the dynamics," Shane said. "Did you?"

A long pause stretched between them before she finally sighed. "Yeah. We tried to start a small auto repair shop. It didn't work out."

"What happened?"

"It went under," Raya muttered.

Shane tilted his head, his tone still gentle. "Who took the hit to their credit?"

Her jaw tightened. "I did. The loan was in my name."

"Why didn't you just pay it off?"

"I didn't have the money," Raya snapped. "Seth was supposed to pay it, but he didn't. He just ... left me to deal with it."

Shane let her words hang in the air for a moment. "If he'd paid you what he owed, your credit would've been fine. Then you and Ronnie could've started your life together, right?"

Raya's lip quivered, and she looked down at her lap. "Yeah," she whispered.

Satisfied for now, Shane changed gears, guiding the conversation back to her parents, noting the shift in her tone when she talked about her mother.

"They were good to us," Raya said, though her voice wavered. "But sometimes it felt like they liked Seth and Missy Ann more. They always got the big Christmas gifts, the good rooms on our family vacations. I got left out because I don't have kids."

"So you think they treated you unfairly?"

Her nod was almost imperceptible, her face suddenly small and vulnerable.

"And then Ronnie came into your life," Shane said, his tone softening. "He gave you the attention you weren't getting from your family."

Her lips twitched into the faintest smile before she tapped it back down. "Yeah. He's the best thing that ever happened to me."

"How'd you meet?"

"Online. He was into gaming, and so am I. We just clicked."

Shane smiled slightly. "What games do you two like to play?"

She listed several, most of them violent strategy games.

"Do you keep any weapons around?"

Her smile faltered. She shook her head slowly. "No. We don't have anything like that."

Shane let the silence stretch before pulling out his notebook. "Your sister said that Ronnie helped your dad out with some of the renovations he was doing in the house. How did that go?"

She shrugged. "Fine, I guess. Ronnie doesn't like that kind of work, but he did it. We needed the money."

"Was he paid well for it?"

"Why? How is that pertinent to the case, Detective?"

Shane pushed his notebook closer to her side of the table and flipped to a photo of Seth's body. "I need you to look at this, Raya. Does anything seem out of place to you around your brother's body?"

Raya only looked a second then turned her head, refusing to look longer. "No," she said quickly.

He flipped to the next page, showing Erin's body.

"I'm really sorry but I need you to do the same with this one."

She looked and her reaction was immediate—a quick flash of anger in her eyes before she looked away.

"What was it about Erin that bothered you so much?" Shane pressed.

"She didn't bother me."

"I'm pretty sure she did, Raya. That's okay—everyone can't be cozy close. Maybe Erin tried too hard to be close to your mom? Pushed you out of the way. It happens in a lot of families."

Raya hesitated, then sighed. "She thought she was better than everyone. Seth was always doing things for her, like I didn't matter anymore. It wasn't fair. Them and their two kids and a dog. Cute house with a fence. Just the picture-perfect family like my mom has always wanted for all her kids. But I let her down. She was ashamed of me."

Shane filed that detail away, then turned to the photos of her parents. Jane, discarded in the shed, her expression frozen into one of disbelief and fear. Willis, sprawled on the ramp with a rolled-up carpet atop him.

Raya visibly flinched when he turned to the autopsy photo of her mother, the body covered to the shoulders with a stark white sheet, on the stainless-steel table. So cold looking and void of life, but, yes, still recognizable.

What was Raya thinking behind her shuttered eyes?

"Raya, your mother will never rest until we figure out who did this," Shane said softly. "Your parents deserve justice. Seth's kids deserve to know why their mommy and daddy will never hug them again. Just think about Nicky and Britney. They lost their mom and dad—and their grandparents. Two innocent kids, their lives shattered forever in one day. Have you seen them? Tried to talk to them?"

Tears welled in Raya's eyes, but she shook her head. "No. I haven't seen them. But I didn't ... I didn't do anything."

"Look at her, Raya. Jane's death was brutal. What would she want you to do now?" He pushed the notebook closer, bumping her arm with it until she looked at her mother's photo.

She winced and he saw her swallow hard before she looked away again.

"Maybe it wasn't your idea," Shane said, his voice barely above a whisper and as comforting as he could make it. "Maybe Ronnie came up with the plan, and you just went along because you were scared. These things happen, Raya. Sometimes two people come together, and they bring out the worst in each other. Apart, they'd never hurt anyone, but together ..."

Her hands clenched into fists, her tears falling freely now. "It wasn't Ronnie," she sobbed, then looked up, locking eyes with him. "It was me. I ... I did it. All of it. I killed them. I'm a monster."

Shane sat back, his heart pounding as her confession spilled out.

Once the sheriff had told him that Timmons had admitted to putting the dog dung in the mailbox but stood firm he'd never been in the house and would take a lie detector test, that had said a lot. Timmon's had most likely left his DNA on a piece of mail, then the mail was transferred to the kitchen counter, leaving a trace of DNA behind.

After Taylor's urgent message to push Raya on the business venture with Seth issue, the rest was easy. That was the best part of playing detective—when all the puzzle pieces started coming together and you knew exactly what you were looking at.

He watched Raya intently and tried to imagine the slight young woman pulling the trigger repeatedly, taking out her family, one by one. If Missy Ann had not canceled and kept her son home, there probably would've been two more victims. Or, another thought, could her presence have done something to stop the blood bath?

They would probably never know.

With her head in her arms on the table, Raya keened now, sounding like a hurt animal. Shane kept his expression calm, letting her sobs fill the room. He felt no sympathy and it was a bit late for crying.

*Suck it up, Raya, it's time to face the music.*

# Chapter Thirty

A few months after Raya's confession, Taylor sat on the bench, on their dock. The lake stretched out before her, shimmering under the unseasonably warm sun. A breeze tousled her hair, and, for the first time in what felt like forever, she truly felt well. She'd even left the cane at home. It was a small victory but a monumental one for her recovery.

Beside her, Sam held a sleeping Lennon in the papoose harnessed around his chest. She would probably stay that way for hours, snuggled against her daddy's warmth, content and snoozing to the beat of his heart. Diesel lay at Taylor's feet, his head on his paws, occasionally twitching at the smell of food wafting through the air.

The dock bustled with life. The table groaned under the weight of fried chicken, potato salad, deviled eggs, and a home-made cake for Cecil's birthday.

Nearby, Brandy lounged beside Cate, keeping her nose pointed in Diesel's direction, both dogs blissfully soaking up the sunshine and happy to have their people sharing outside time with them.

The kids fished from the end of the dock, their laughter

carrying over the water as they shouted about the elusive striper fish they were determined to catch. Levi was usually the champion fisherman, and he looked serious as a heart attack.

Johnny tried with them and he looked hot but happy, his chubby cheeks red and his plump little arms like sausages protruding from the life jacket he wore.

Taylor noticed Cate and Ellis huddled together at one side of the table. Jo stood with her arm around Levi, and Anna was trying—and failing—to corral her Chihuahua, Mutt, as Johnny waved his fishing pole over the tiny dog, the hook swinging dangerously close to his muzzle. Mutt was doing well, considering he'd lost his best friend, Jeff, the Great Dane, the year before. It had taken some weeks of grieving where he'd stayed nonstop in the dog bed he'd shared with Jeff, as if waiting for him to return, but finally he was himself again.

"Johnny, no!" Anna shrieked, her voice lilting with panic as Mutt darted between the tables. The little dog skittered under the bench, but Johnny was determined. He dropped the fishing pole and crouched low, his chubby hands outstretched, and made a grab for Mutt's tail.

The Chihuahua yelped, spun around, and barked furiously.

Johnny froze, his big eyes blinking in surprise before he let out a giggle that sent the adults into peals of laughter from Bronwyn, Teague, and Levi.

"Poor Mutt," Alice said.

"Johnny, stop terrorizing that poor dog!" Taylor called, unable to keep the smile off her face. Johnny wouldn't really hurt him. He loved all the dogs.

"Mutt's going to need therapy after this," Anna muttered, scooping up the trembling dog and glaring playfully at her nephew. It was amusing to see Anna so crazy over a dog when, for so many years, she had no interest in animals.

"Maybe he'll think twice before stealing Johnny's bait again," Sam quipped, earning a round of chuckles.

As the laughter faded, the conversation took a more somber turn. Corbin, seated at the edge of the picnic table with Sutton, glanced at Taylor. "So, about this Colburn case," he began, his voice tentative. "I've been reading up on it. What kind of person does something like that?"

Taylor's smile faded. She shifted, folding her arms across her chest. Since Raya Colburn's confession and all the media surrounding it, others had come forward with stories. People from the apartment complex she'd once lived in declaring that Raya would fall into a fit of screaming and hysteria if anyone accidentally took her parking space, or if a neighbor's cat crossed her patio. Her coworkers claimed that Raya acted like a spoiled child if she didn't get the exact schedule she wanted, or if her till came up short, and she'd blame everyone but herself.

A distant cousin recalled a visit the year before when he was watching a football game with Jane and Willis, and Raya had come in and demanded money to put tires on her car. That his aunt and uncle had said no but Raya had finally worn them down, until Jane wrote a check.

Missy Ann had known that her little sister was taking advantage of her parents financially, but had no idea the extent of it until everything came out.

"She was a bully and a coward," Taylor said simply.

"What about the boyfriend?" Sutton asked, leaning forward. "Randy something?"

"Ronnie. Ronnie McGill," Sam added.

Taylor sighed. "I have no pity for him. In his interview, he had the gall to say, 'I'm sorry that they're gone. They were my family, too, you know?'"

"If he'd have been any kind of man, the first time Raya

brought up the idea of killing her family, he would've gone to her parents and told them that she needed help."

"He's just as evil as she is," Anna said.

Ellis, who had been silent until now, frowned. "I heard Raya actually asked for the death penalty at one point. Her lawyers had to talk her out of it when she finally told them the truth, that Ronnie was the actual executioner, when her own gun had failed. But it was all done under her bidding, no matter who pulled the trigger."

The group fell quiet for a moment, the weight of the tragedy settling over them.

"It's eerie," Cate said softly, her hand resting on Ellis's arm. "That someone could be that angry, that misguided to that extent, and no one noticed. So much jealousy brewing over how she thought her siblings were preferred over her. Then, in one day, a whole family is gone."

Cecil, the birthday boy himself, shook his head. "And at Christmas, no less. When the rest of the world is pausing for kindness, compassion, and renewing bonds with loved ones. It's a cruelty I'll never understand."

Cate nodded, her expression thoughtful. "That's why the world needs Christmas. The twinkling lights, the food, the gifts —the love we trade to distract us from all the stress and troubles of the year. But now, Missy Ann and Justin—and Seth and Erin's kids—will never feel that holiday cheer again. Every year, it'll just be a reminder of what they lost."

Sam's jaw tightened, and he shook his head. "It shows just how callous Raya is. To plan the murder for that specific day makes me realize even more that devils walk among us, hiding in plain sight until they can't contain their evil thoughts anymore."

The mood was plummeting fast and Taylor held up a hand. "Okay, let's move this conversation somewhere else. Jo, is Lucy coming down?"

Jo glanced toward the cabins, though the trees obscured her view. "I think so. Before she got into the shower, she said she was. Said she wanted Ginger to have some playtime with the other dogs."

Anna scoffed. "You would think that she'd be more worried about spending time with Johnny. She's so selfish. Just like she says she still can't live alone. She needs to give Levi his space back and stop being such a baby."

Taylor was about to divert the topic once again, but Corbin broke the tension with a grin. "By the way, I had a small gig at a bar in Nashville last week. Just warming up, but it's helping me get over my stage fright. Only works if Sutton's there, though."

Sutton swatted his arm. "Stop being such a charmer! You've got tons of women falling for your lines."

He chuckled. "Maybe, but you're the only one for me."

She blushed, shaking her head. "You're impossible."

Sam, never one to miss an opportunity to tease, leaned forward. "You better put a ring on it, Corbin. Sutton's the best thing that's ever happened to you."

Ellis laughed. "Speaking of rings, my daughter just informed me that the resort she's holding her wedding at in Cabo is an all-inclusive, adults-only resort. They'd planned all sorts of things for the wedding party; a white party on a yacht, golfing and a whiskey tour for the guys, spa day for the girls, camel-riding ..."

Taylor grimaced. "I don't know if any of us can manage that. No one wants to leave the kids for a whole week, especially Lennon."

Cate leaned over to whisper, "We'll figure something out for Lennon because I'm going to need you there, Taylor. You know his kids hate me, and I'm sure their family still thinks I'm some kind of low-class gold digger."

Taylor squeezed her mom's arm. "Mom, I bet that's not true."

Suddenly, the sound of a car engine peeling out on gravel up toward the farm shattered the moment. Everyone looked up, confused.

"Who was that?" Jo asked, standing to get a better view.

Taylor frowned. "I'll go check." Cate stood with her, and the two made their way back up the path.

"Lucy's car isn't at Jo's cabin," Cate said, shielding her eyes against the sun.

"Where would she be going?" Taylor mused.

They walked up to Jo's cabin and went inside. When they didn't see Lucy or her dog, Ginger, they walked back to Levi's bedroom. The bed was unmade, and clothes were scattered all over the floor.

Taylor went into his bathroom. "Mom? All her toiletries are gone."

"Maybe she moved back into her own cabin," Cate said. "Let's go look."

When they reached Lucy's cabin, they found the door ajar. Inside her bedroom, drawers were open, clothes scattered across the floor. A lot was gone—her clothes, her shoes, even her dog.

Taylor rushed to Lucy's bathroom and saw medicine bottles lined up behind the faucet. She picked one up and shook it. It was nearly full. She felt like the earth moved, making her feel sick at her stomach.

"She didn't take her meds," she whispered as Cate came in.

Lucy had made big improvements since they'd found the right medication and dosage to keep her leveled out, but this appeared she hadn't been taking them after all and had set the bottles out as a declaration.

"That's not good," Cate said.

They went back through the house and, in the living room,

right on the coffee table, a note was left behind. How they'd missed it the first time around was beyond Taylor.

*"Don't try to find me. The mice are back."*

She sank onto the couch, tears stinging her eyes. Lucy was still paranoid. Probably completely out of her head. Anger rose. "She took Ginger with her but couldn't be bothered to take Johnny?"

Cate placed a comforting hand on her shoulder. "I know this is hard, Taylor, but, if you ask me, it's the biggest compliment that Lucy could give you. She trusts you with her son more than she trusts herself right now. She knows you'll keep him safe. That we all will"

Taylor bit her lip, her anger giving way to fear. "What if something happens to her? She needs medical intervention. She needs her medication."

"Yes, but Lucy is tough," her mother assured her. "She's lived on the streets before, without a penny to her name. At least now she has resources. She'll be fine, and she'll come back. She wouldn't have left Johnny otherwise."

Taylor nodded, but the ache in her chest didn't ease. Once again, Lucy was gone again, and that meant that, until she resurfaced, a part of Taylor's heart was ripped out of her chest, ragged and hurting.

# Chapter Thirty-One

"I know I can't be there, but remember this, Taylor," Alice had said as she'd seen Taylor to the car earlier that morning. Of course, she knew about the Colburns and unfortunately also the grisly details. A middle-schooler with a smart phone had a handle on current events.

Her feisty stepdaughter had looked defiant as she stood by the car window. "A famous author named Lois McMaster Bujold said that 'the dead cannot cry out for justice. That it is the duty of the living to do so for them.'"

"Thanks, honey," Taylor said, then pulled away from the driveway, out the gates and down to the square in town.

Alice—*and Bujold*—was so right. At least Taylor hoped so, and that, when the trial was said and done, justice truly would prevail for the Colburns.

Once in the building, a movement caught Taylor's eye, and she recognized Nancy Hurst, Erin's mother, sitting on the bench outside the courtroom. She was the one who had stumbled onto the murder scene, and had unfortunately seen all four bodies, including that of her daughter. She would be called as a witness, therefore couldn't be there during the proceedings.

"I'm so very sorry, Mrs. Hurst," Taylor said softly when she got close enough.

Nancy nodded. She looked strong and in control. She'd probably be there every single day, sitting just outside as the trial moved from day to day, taking her daughter's memory through the wringer.

"Thank you," Nancy said. It came out like she'd said it a few thousand times that day alone, and the words were written on her face, automatic on her tongue.

Taylor slipped quietly into the courtroom, the heavy oak door creaking as it closed behind her. The air was dense with anticipation, the hum of whispered conversations fading as Judge Crawford took his place at the bench. Shane was seated confidently behind the prosecution's table, his profile sharp and proud. His posture radiated the confidence of a man who believed he'd solved the case, and for good reason.

Of course he didn't turn to look for her. She would be the last thing on his mind.

Special Agents Maeve Hanson and Jared Tuffin from the Georgia Bureau of Investigation sat in the same row as Shane.

Her chest tightened. A pang of something close to jealousy flickered through her. She hadn't done much in the case—just a few quiet nudges in the right direction, connecting the dots on Raya's anger about money that fueled it all. But she couldn't shake the feeling of being sidelined, as though her contributions didn't matter.

She took a seat at the back, careful to not disturb the court. Cate and Ellis had the kids until the afternoon, leaving her free to be here, to witness the beginning of justice for Jane and Willis, and Seth and Erin ... to begin its slow march forward. She wouldn't stay long, just a half hour or so, then back to the farm.

Sam was there now, working in his shop, only a text away if

Quig needed him. On that note, he'd taken the news pretty well when Taylor had advised him that they would have an additional child under their roof indefinitely. He'd shrugged, saying, "The more the merrier," and hugged her tightly, easing her anxiety about telling him, though he couldn't lift the worry she held over where Lucy was and if she was okay.

Prosecutor Lance Hamilton rose to address the jury, and Taylor's attention shifted. His voice was calm, deliberate, as he painted a holiday tableau for the jurors.

"Ladies and gentlemen, imagine this: Christmas Eve in a quiet, wooded home. A tree adorned with lights, a roast in the oven. Jane Colburn wrapping gifts for her grandchildren while her husband, Willis, relaxes in his favorite chair. A family preparing for the holiday season."

The courtroom was silent, save for the faint scratch of a pen as a juror jotted notes on a legal pad. Taylor leaned back in her seat, letting the details wash over her. It was hard to reconcile the peaceful image, knowing the brutality that followed.

"In an instant, everything changed," Hamilton continued, his voice dropping an octave, before the dramatic next words. "When Raya Colburn and her boyfriend, Ronnie McGill, entered that home."

Taylor's gaze flickered toward the defense table, where Raya sat with her head bowed. Her dark hair hung like a curtain, obscuring her face, but her body seemed unnaturally still. It was almost as though she had already resigned herself to her fate.

In stark contrast, Missy Ann sat a few rows ahead of Taylor and to the left, close to the front. Tears streaked her face, her lips trembling as she stared at her younger sister. The look in her eyes was accusatory, raw, as though she couldn't fully process the monster Raya had become.

Taylor had heard whispers about the confrontation in jail—how Missy Ann had demanded answers, had pleaded with Raya to explain why she'd destroyed their family. It had been emotional, an explosion of grief and anger, and, afterward, Missy Ann had cut all ties.

They hadn't spoken since.

Taylor's chest tightened as she watched the older sister now, her shoulders trembling as she silently wept. She couldn't imagine what it would feel like to lose so much in one instant—and, worse, to lose it at the hands of someone you'd shared your childhood with. Someone you thought you could trust.

Family. Your own blood, even. Did Missy Ann now wonder if she herself had the capability to be a cold-blooded killer?

Taylor's thoughts shifted to her own sisters. Growing up, she'd believed she knew them better than anyone else in the world. Their secrets, their quirks, their dreams. But watching Missy Ann, she now realized how little people truly knew about one another, even within a family.

What must it be like to discover that someone you thought you understood—someone you thought you loved—was capable of such unimaginable cruelty?

Take Lucy, for example. Taylor had thought that Johnny was her sister's most prized achievement, her reason to better herself and work hard to be successful. Even her reason for living! Never in a million years did she think Lucy could just up and disappear, leaving him behind to wonder where his mom was. He'd had a lot of teary-eyed nights over the last few months, asking for his mommy when he was sleepy and exhausted, needing to feel her presence.

Thankfully, he was doing much better, but there was no telling what was going on in his little head, what trauma Lucy had caused him, that he would carry forward into his life. It was just inconceivable that her sister would do this to him, especially after the childhood trauma that they had all survived. Didn't she want different for Johnny?

Couldn't she see what she was doing to him? To all of them?

She returned her focus to Hamilton, who was now outlining the grim sequence of events.

"Greed," he said, his voice sharp. "That's what this is about. Pure, unadulterated greed. Raya Colburn didn't just want more —she believed she was entitled to it. She believed her parents, her brother, they all owed her something. And when they didn't deliver, she took matters into her own hands."

Taylor straightened, a small flicker of validation washing over her. She'd seen it first—that thread of entitlement woven through Raya's story. Her resentment toward Seth, her anger over money she believed was hers.

"Poor Erin Colburn, wife to Seth and mother of two young children, Nicky and Britney. The crime scene dictated that, out of everyone, she'd been especially brutalized. And why? I'll tell you why—because she was married to Seth. Miss Colburn was jealous of losing her brother's attention. And she was jealous that Erin was everything she wasn't. A good wife. A mother. A caring and attentive daughter-in-law, stepping into the shoes that Raya couldn't fill."

He then laid it all out: the meticulous planning, the cold calculation, the lengths to which Raya Colburn and Ronnie McGill had gone to cover their tracks. Photos of the wooded property and the house were shown, and then the crime scenes themselves, but Taylor couldn't bring herself to look. She'd already seen them and wanted those visions to fade from her memory.

Instead, her gaze drifted to Raya again. She hadn't moved, hadn't even flinched at the descriptions of the murders.

Missy Ann, on the other hand, was visibly shaking, her hands clenched tightly in her lap. Taylor could almost feel the waves of grief and fury radiating from her.

"Raya Colburn believed she deserved more," Hamilton

concluded, his voice steady. "But what she did was not justifiable. It was not excusable. The death bullets may not have come from her gun but were surely fired by her orders. Raya Colburn convinced Ronnie McGill that her family members were evil, that they'd always picked on her. That they should pay for her long years of feeling neglected and abused. She worked on him for three weeks, planning every last detail leading up to Christmas Eve. What Raya did that day was no less than cold, calculated murder, driven by selfishness and greed. And we will prove that to you in the weeks ahead."

As Hamilton returned to his seat, Judge Crawford called for a recess. The courtroom erupted into soft murmurs as people began to stand, stretch, or leave their seats.

Taylor stayed put, her eyes locked on Shane. He was still seated behind the prosecution's table, his shoulders back, his expression unreadable. She wondered what he was thinking. Relief? Pride? Did he feel the weight of the case on his shoulders or the exhilaration of having cracked it?

She thought about telling the sheriff what she'd done, the small ways she'd helped Shane get to the end of the investigation. But she knew better.

Dawkins would only see her involvement as disobeying direct orders from him, call it reckless. Admitting the truth might cost her the fragile trust they'd been building. He and the doctor had both agreed that she was almost ready to go back to work. Taylor didn't want to jeopardize it. She planned on telling Sam that evening, just to give him time to mentally prepare, and so that they could discuss what it meant for Lennon and Johnny.

As the prosecutor continued, Taylor quietly slipped out, her mind churning as she thought about the thin, fragile threads that bound families together, and how easily they could snap. She'd spent most of her life trying to keep her family ties tightened and keep her loved ones safe. Sometimes the lines were flimsy, but, so far, always there. She had no plans to relax her sentry now.

\* \* \*

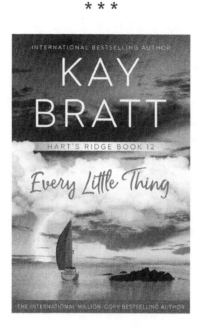

## A NOTE FROM THE AUTHOR

Hello, readers! I hope you enjoyed So This is Christmas, the eleventh book in the *Hart's Ridge* series. The true crime wrapped into the fictional town of Hart's Ridge and its fictional characters was very loosely inspired by the Carnation murders of Judy and Wayne Anderson, their son and daughter-in-law, Scott and Erica, and the grandchildren, Olivia and Nathan, five and three years old. As you may have noticed, I couldn't bear to write the children's heartbreaking deaths into my story. My deepest condolences go out to the family for this senseless tragedy. Writing about murder set in Christmastime is not something I ever saw myself doing, but perhaps, just like me, some of you embrace the truth, that there is always danger lurking, waiting to rear its ugly head, even in times that are supposed to be full of peace and love.

On another note, guess what? I've got a bonus chapter for you! It's from the last book, *Hello Little Girl*, and picks up after Lydia comes home. I think you'll like this short peek into their holiday. Keep scrolling to find it!

Also, if you've enjoyed the eleven books of Hart's Ridge thus far, you'll be happy to know that I've decided to continue the series. Next up is **Every Little Thing**. Just look at the beautiful cover!

You've probably guessed, by the sailboat and gorgeous sunset, that you as a reader are cordially invited to attend the wedding of Ellis' daughter, to be held on the grounds of the all-inclusive high-end resort in Cabo San Lucas, Mexico. Cate feels like an outsider, especially since Ellis' daughter is not too fond of her new stepmother. To give her mother emotional support, Taylor (and Sam) will be attending, and let's just say the term, 'til death do we part, might take on a whole new warning—oops, meaning. If you'd like to be notified when there is a publish date for **Every Little Thing**, you can be among the first to know when you sign up for my monthly newsletter at the following link:

## JOIN KAY'S NEWSLETTER HERE

While you're waiting on the next book in this series, I have many more books for you to read! I'd love for you to check out my bestselling *By The Sea* trilogy, starting with True to Me, a mystery with lots of family drama that packs a heck of a twist!

Nearly 13,000 Amazon Reviews can give you some insight on why it's a fan favorite! (See cover and book description below)

I'd also like to invite you to join my private Facebook group, Kay's Krew, where you can be part of my focus group, giving ideas for story details such as names, livelihoods, and get sneak peeks for this series. I'm also known to entertain with stories of my life with the Bratt Pack and all the kerfuffles I find myself getting into. Please join my author newsletter to hear of future Hart's Ridge books, as well as giveaways and discounts.

Until then,

Scatter kindness everywhere.

Kay Bratt

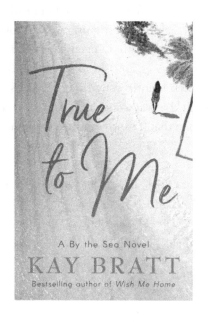

*Learn More about True to Me at this link: My Book or keep scrolling to see the book description:

· · ·

**From the bestselling author of *Wish Me Home* comes a breathtaking novel about the secrets that families keep and one woman's illuminating search for the truth.**

Quinn Maguire has a stable life, a fiancé and what she thinks is a clear vision for her future. All of that comes undone by her mother's deathbed confession—the absentee father Quinn spent thirty years resenting is not her real father at all. With that one revealing whisper, Quinn embarks on a journey to Maui, her mother's childhood home, a storied paradise that holds the truth about her mother's past and all its secrets Quinn is determined to uncover.

But settling on the island has its complications, and, with the fiancé she left behind questioning every choice she makes, Quinn's quest for her truth is even more difficult than she expected. As time passes and she digs deeper into her family history and her own identity, one thing becomes clear: Maui is as beautiful as she'd always imagined, and its magic is helping uncover the woman that Quinn was always meant to be.

Get True to Me in eBook, Paperback, and Audio here:

My Book
Want to read a sneak peek of **True To Me**? Keep turning the pages, but first ...

## LYDIA & CALEB BONUS CHAPTER

The fire crackled low, embers glowing orange against the soft Florida night. Caleb Grimes leaned back in his camping chair, the warm breeze carrying the tang of salt from the nearby Gulf. The air felt strange for Christmas—too warm, too easy—but this was what the girls had wanted. A break from the cold, from the heaviness of their year, and he couldn't blame them.

They'd picked up an old motor home, trading his truck and some cash for it. He couldn't say it was luxurious, but, with some sweat equity and Lydia's touches, it was their home on wheels, and a real blessing.

Grace and Ella sat cross-legged on the ground, sticks in hand as they skewered marshmallows over the fire. Little Zoey, with her hair a wild halo of curls, giggled on Lydia's lap, sticky fingers clutching half a graham cracker. Caleb tried to focus on the scene in front of him, tried to lock it away in his memory like a keepsake. But his eyes kept drifting to Lydia.

She looked beautiful in the firelight, the shadows softening the angles of her face, hiding every hint of the trauma she'd endured. Her laugh rang out, light and unburdened, as Zoey tried to smush the cracker into her marshmallow. It was a sound he thought he'd never hear again.

Because, for a time, she was gone.

His chest tightened at the memory, his hand tightening on the beer can resting against his knee. Gone wasn't the word for it. Stolen. Kidnapped. Ripped away from him by a man whose darkness Caleb had underestimated.

Norman Addler.

He was gone but the name still sent a ripple of anger through him, even now, with Lydia back at his side. Back where she belonged. Caleb tipped his head back and stared up at the stars. He should've seen it coming. That night years ago, showing up to the domestic call, he'd seen the hate in Addler's eyes. And then later, when his wife left him, Addler had made a new target for his rage. Caleb's family.

He had taken Lydia.

The guilt was a low thrum in Caleb's chest that never fully went away. He was the reason Addler had fixated on her. The reason she'd endured the unthinkable. And though she was here now, her laugh floating through the warm night, the shadows of what she'd been through still lingered, etched into her in ways he could barely understand.

He couldn't imagine the scars she wore that none of them could see. The scars they all would've worn had she not returned to them.

They'd met Shara Williams' family and had turned over the ashes to the never forgotten daughter who'd vanished without a trace so many decades before. Stolen and made to live a life of fear, first from her abductor, then her own son, Norman.

Shara's father had died ten or so years before, but they'd found her mother still holding on, trying to live until she knew what had happened to her daughter.

Now she knew, and Caleb bet the woman wouldn't last another month. While the news wasn't what she'd hoped for, at least now her daughter was at peace and that meant she could be, too.

"Earth to Dad."

Grace's voice snapped him out of his thoughts. She grinned at him, holding up a perfectly golden marshmallow. "You want one, or are you too busy zoning out?"

He forced a smile. "I'll take one. You gonna make me the perfect s'more, or do I have to do the hard part?"

Grace rolled her eyes but handed him the marshmallow. "Here. I guess you earned it."

He chuckled and started assembling his s'more, glancing over at Lydia again. She caught him looking and smiled softly, her eyes full of understanding. She always seemed to know when his mind drifted back to those months without her. The months where he'd torn apart half the state looking for her, only to come up empty-handed, people trying to convince him she was dead.

Caleb had never given up. His throat tightened as he thought about what she'd gone through. Her sheer strength. Her will to survive. He was supposed to be the one to save her, but Lydia had found her own way out, and, in the end, he'd only been there to pick up the pieces.

Soon he'd have to return to Hart's Ridge. To his job with the department.

He sighed heavily.

"Caleb," she said quietly, drawing his attention. Zoey had wriggled off her lap and was toddling toward Ella, who held out a marshmallow in her direction. Lydia's gaze locked on his, a hint of concern there. "You okay?"

He nodded, swallowing the lump in his throat. "Yeah. Just ... thinking."

"About going back?"

Her words hit him like a punch to the gut. She always knew what was on his mind, but he didn't want to ruin the night. Didn't want to admit that the thought of returning to law enforcement filled him with anxiety he couldn't shake.

How could he go back to chasing down men like Addler? Every call would remind him of what he'd nearly lost.

"Yeah," he admitted finally, his voice low.

Lydia leaned forward, resting her hand over his. Her touch was warm, grounding him. "You don't have to decide anything yet," she said softly.

But he did, didn't he? They were living on their already-meager savings. He couldn't stay out of work forever, couldn't keep running from the job he'd spent his life doing. And yet the thought of leaving Lydia, even for a shift, made his chest tighten with panic.

"I don't want to leave you," he said quietly. "Not for twelve hour shifts. Not for eight. Not for even one."

"Well, you're not doing it right now so stop borrowing trouble," she said, her voice steady. "We're here right now. Together. That's what matters."

He nodded, squeezing her hand, but his mind was already racing. What kind of man would he be if he couldn't protect the people he loved? And how could he keep doing a job he dreaded doing, without losing himself in the process?

The fire popped, sending a spray of sparks into the air. Grace laughed at something Ella said, and Zoey squealed with delight as her marshmallow dripped into the dirt. Caleb looked around at his family, his heart full and aching all at once.

He didn't know what the future held, but, for now, he was holding on to this moment. This night. And maybe, just maybe, they could find a way to build something better.

* * *

Lydia held Zoey's hand tightly as they crossed the parking lot, the neon glow of the Krispy Kreme sign lighting up the night. The smell of hot sugar and fried dough wafted through the air, bringing a rare sense of peace. Inside, the girls chattered about the show they'd just seen, their voices overlapping in excitement.

"That part where Ebony Scrooge was singing her solo?" Grace exclaimed, her face flushed with enthusiasm. "Chills. Actual chills."

"I loved how the music just pulled you in," Ella added, her hands waving in the air. "Like, gospel and Christmas? Perfect mix."

Zoey skipped along beside Lydia, humming a tune that vaguely resembled one from the show. Even Caleb, usually stoic these days, had been humming under his breath as they walked to the car.

The theatre performance had been more than just entertainment. It was joy. Connection. A reminder of everything Lydia had fought to come back to.

The warmth of the doughnut shop embraced them as they stepped inside. Caleb ordered hot doughnuts and cocoa for everyone, while Lydia led the girls to a corner table. They slid into the seats, Zoey climbing onto her lap. Lydia couldn't help but marvel at the ordinary scene.

It was hard to believe she was here, in this moment. Not in a basement. Not in that shelter. Not scraping by each day, one second at a time, desperate to see and hold her children again. They were within reach, and, if she could get by with it, she'd tie them all to her and never let them out of her sight again.

The contrast hit her like it always did—a jarring collision of what was and what could have been. For months, she'd woken up expecting to find herself back there, her freedom a cruel dream. So many nightmares. But tonight, surrounded by her family, laughter, and the smell of hot doughnuts, it felt almost ... real.

Almost.

She hadn't admitted it to anyone, but at times she had to fight against her thoughts, the ones that told her this was the dream, that she was really back in the shelter and, when she woke up, all this joy would be gone, and she'd only have Jill.

She wondered how the girl was getting along. They'd promised to stay in touch but Gwen, her mother, probably didn't want Lydia to be a reminder to her daughter of the time she'd spent in captivity.

Caleb returned with a tray laden with cocoa and doughnuts, and the girls cheered. He set the tray down, his eyes catching hers for a brief moment, and she saw the same wonder reflected there.

As they dug in, Lydia sipped her cocoa and let the moment settle. She watched Caleb, his brow furrowed in that way it did when his thoughts weighed heavy, and she knew what he was thinking. She always knew.

"Hey," she said softly, breaking into the stream of conversation. All three girls turned to her. "I've been thinking about something."

Caleb arched a brow, pausing mid-bite.

"Oh no," Grace said, grinning. "Mom's got ideas."

"Hey—Mom's ideas are usually good," Ella said with a teasing shrug.

"Well, I was thinking about tonight," Lydia began. She glanced at Caleb, then back to the girls. "How much fun we had. And how it wasn't just the show, but being together. No phones, no distractions. Just ... us."

The girls nodded. Caleb leaned back in his chair, his expression unreadable.

"What if," Lydia continued, her words gaining momentum, "we could give other families the same kind of experience? A chance to step away from the craziness of life, reconnect, and just ... breathe?"

Grace tilted her head. "Like a retreat?"

"Not a fancy one," Lydia said quickly, catching Caleb's doubtful look. "Something simple. Like a family camp. Cabins, outdoor activities, time to just be together."

Zoey piped up, "Can we have s'mores?"

"Absolutely," Lydia said, smiling.

Ella's eyes lit up. "And scavenger hunts. Or obstacle courses! Oh, and a lake for swimming."

Grace nodded enthusiastically. "And cooking classes."

"I agree," Lydia said. "Classes or challenges with families

working together to make meals. Coming together over the table again. I miss that so much and never appreciated it enough until it was taken from me."

Caleb stayed quiet, his arms crossed as he watched the girls.

Lydia could see the flicker of hesitation in his eyes, the weight of practicality.

"It doesn't have to be huge," Lydia said, addressing him directly. "We could start small. A couple of cabins, maybe a central lodge for group activities. A few RV hookups, maybe? Hart's Ridge already gets tourists. This could be something different—focused on families, on connection."

"And where exactly are we getting the money for this?" Caleb asked, though his tone was less skeptical than she expected.

"We could start with fundraising," Grace offered. "Like hosting community events. A Christmas festival, maybe?"

"And we could apply for grants," Ella added. "There have to be programs that support things like this."

"Plus, you know the whole town would pitch in," Lydia said. "They've been behind us through everything. This could be a project for healing. I think so many people would see it the same way and step up to help us make this dream come true."

Caleb looked around the table, his gaze lingering on each of them. Lydia could see the idea taking root, the doubt giving way to curiosity.

"I don't know," he said finally, his voice soft. "It's ... a lot."

"So was this year," Lydia said gently. "A lot, I mean. No one predicted this outcome, did they? But we made it through and here we are. Together, we can do anything we set our minds to. We've proved that, Caleb."

The girls nodded in unison, their excitement palpable. Even Zoey chimed in, though her contribution was mostly about s'mores.

Caleb sighed, but a small smile tugged at the corner of his mouth. "You said 'dream.' Is this really your dream to do this?"

Lydia reached across the table and took his hand. "It is now. I've already got a name for it. *Camp Hart.*"

He chuckled. "Of course you do."

"I love it," Ella said, clapping her hands. Zoey clapped hers, too, just to be included. The glaze from her hands flew in all directions, and they all laughed.

Caleb sighed. "I'm not saying yes right now, at this moment. But I am saying let's get some of these ideas down on paper. Costs, too. Look at land for sale around Hart's Ridge. And if we determine it's all doable, then we go for it."

"I knew you'd see things my way," Lydia joked, squeezing his hand before dropping it to put half a donut in her mouth. She didn't care about calories and love handles any longer. If the last year had taught her anything, it was to stop sweating the small stuff and just live ... to love, laugh, and be together.

"Can we see that show again before we leave here? This town?" Ella asked.

As the conversation shifted back to the show and their plans for the next leg of their trip, Lydia allowed herself a moment to dream. The family camp wasn't just an idea; it was a way forward. A way to turn pain into purpose. And maybe, just maybe, it was exactly what they all needed. \*\*\*

True To Me
Chapter One Sneak Peek

Quinn held the small box in her hands, so focused on the contents that even the busy Savannah traffic outside the condo couldn't penetrate her thoughts. The box felt weightless. Other than the tiny molecules painted on the side, it was plain and unassuming.

But it could be the link to her future.

Or her past.

At this point in her life, both were uncertain.

The only thing she knew for sure was that she needed to begin living again. Before she could do that, she needed to put her mother to rest. In her latest self-help book, she'd read that grief never ends, but it changes. That it's a passage, and not a place to stay. Quinn needed to pull herself out of the pit of sorrow she'd been living in before she drowned in it.

An hour earlier, she'd watched the final episode in the latest season of *Long-Lost Family*, a series that highlighted family reunions between people who'd never met, and she couldn't help but think of what results the small box could bring to her own life.

After checking the activation code, she scanned the terms and conditions, noting that whether she was pleased with the results or not, she couldn't sue. That meant even if they turned up a serial killer for a father, too bad, the company wasn't responsible. The consent form was especially entertaining, asking for her signature *to better understand the human species.*

Quinn could definitely use some assistance in that department.

She filled the small tube with her saliva and capped it. The motion felt strange. Sterile. Such a scientific method for an enormously emotional subject. Quickly, before she could change her mind again, she dropped it into the envelope and sealed it shut, then packed it back into the box. Tomorrow she'd drop it off on her way to work.

Her heart thumped in her chest, beginning the countdown. One second gone, two seconds, three. The waiting would feel endless. But hadn't she already waited her entire life? What was a few more weeks?

This was it. If all went well, it could mean the end to a lifetime of wondering and longing. *Weeks,* the advertisement said. In only weeks she would, or could—or maybe only possibly—have a match. A match didn't necessarily mean she would have what she needed dropped into her hands. Possibly not names, or even explanations. But it meant information. Information could lead to the truth, and the truth to her father.

Her stable, comfortable life had turned complicated. How does a woman come to grips with the fact that the mother she'd known and loved for thirty years had kept such a huge secret from her?

It was a slow progression from the onset of illness to her mother's death. Quinn had been there for her as much as any daughter possibly could. There had been time. More than enough time. So why had her mother waited until her very last moments to confess?

*"Wesley Maguire isn't your father,"* she'd whispered, holding Quinn's hand to her face before telling Quinn her final wish. *"Take me back to Maui."*

In her shock, Quinn hadn't had time to process the proclamation, much less to ask if he wasn't her father, then who was? The confession was startling, and her mother's eyes had begged for forgiveness, even as the light in them faded away.

The weeks that followed were heavy with grief, and in the moments when Quinn could set her sadness aside briefly, she'd searched through every document she could find in her mother's apartment, sorting through the tangled yet mundane details of a life now gone.

While part of her struggled through the realization that she was truly alone in the world—or at least had no family to speak of—the other part of her felt the need to find some clue as to who her real father was. And why had her mother kept it a secret? To give herself the illusion she wasn't behaving obsessively or erratically, she told herself that she was simply putting her mother's affairs in order—ripping off the Band-Aid before she even had a chance to heal.

With an intensity that would make her fiancé, Ethan, proud, Quinn sorted through years of hospital bills and treatment summaries. Lists of medications and books filled with fantasies of alternative medicines.

Receipts. So many receipts. At the end, her mother had made sure to leave no bills behind for Quinn to have to deal with. No unpaid mortgage or car loans. No outstanding medical bills. All of it prepaid, even with a cushion in case she dragged on longer than the doctors predicted.

How strange that she would receive a credit on the cost of her mother's death. That was something she couldn't even begin to process.

After all the medical and business papers were dealt with and organized, she started on the boxes stashed under her mother's bed, sure that there she'd find a clue. Instead she found box after box of old pictures, school papers, and crafts. Her mother had kept everything. It took hours, but Quinn looked through stacks of photos of her life from kindergarten until college graduation, many of them of her and Maggie, her best friend from childhood.

She picked up one and smiled. In the shot the sun shone down on Maggie's hair, making it almost seem to be on fire, a red that flamed bright in her younger years before it began to lighten. The contrast between the two of them was evident— Quinn's golden brown, native Hawaiian skin a startling contrast to Maggie's pale, freckled face.

Putting the photo aside, she dug deeper through brittle corsages and ticket stubs from the many events they'd attended together. So many memories, but nothing from her mother's earlier past.

Quinn persisted.

She started on her mother's jewelry box next, separating out the costume pieces to see if there was anything of value. She found a diamond stud earring but couldn't find the match to it. Finally, she emptied the box and turned it over, and when she saw that one of the corners had come loose at the bottom, she pulled it and realized it was a false bottom.

Underneath was a single photograph.

In the picture, two young women dressed in graduation caps and gowns sat astride horses, their closeness evident in their body language and expressions. Even through the adolescent features, Quinn could tell one of them was definitely her mother. She turned the photo over and saw *Carmen Crowe and Me* scribbled on it with a date of a year before Quinn was born.

Who was Carmen Crowe?

Quinn wished she'd pushed her mother more to talk about the past. Over the years, as Quinn grew older and more curious, her mom had only told her that Maui was a beautiful and magical place, but her childhood had been ugly. The few times Quinn had tried to squeeze more out of her had caused her mother to retreat into silence. It was clear that her mom had loved Maui, but whatever it was that had kept her from returning there must've been traumatic. Quinn had hoped one day her mother would be ready to talk about it.

That day never came.

But if Quinn could find this hopefully living, breathing person from the photo, it could help her find out something about her mother. Carmen was obviously someone important. Important enough that it was the only photo of her past she'd saved. So was she a best friend? Cousin?

As though her mother's death wasn't hard enough to get over, Quinn was also spiraling because of the quietly explosive way she'd left. She couldn't quite believe it or even process it. Not that Quinn had known her father at all, but it was still mind-boggling that she'd spent her life resenting the wrong man. All she knew was the man she'd thought was her father, Wesley Maguire, was someone her mother had been with for a short time many years ago. When they'd parted ways, Quinn was the only thing left of their relationship.

She'd been too young to remember him, but her mother had tried to reach out to him occasionally. As a young girl, Quinn had dreams that he'd show up at her door, ready to take her to the annual Daddy-Daughter Dance, holding a bouquet of flowers and apologizing for taking so long. He would be tall and good-looking, his eyes sparkling down at her with pride.

That never happened, but she'd still held out hope that he'd find her again in time to attend her high school graduation.

That didn't happen either.

By the time Quinn was in college, she'd given up thinking he'd magically appear to walk her down the aisle on her eventual wedding day. And now her mother's words echoed through her head at least a hundred times a day.

*Wesley Maguire is not your father.*

After the dust settled and the impact of that statement had finally worked its way through her brain, Quinn still couldn't hate her for it. The truth was, she would miss her mother so much. Already missed her. Her mom had been kind and loving, completely devoted to Quinn. Whatever she'd done or whatever secrets she'd kept, there was no doubt it was out of love. Now that her mother was gone and Quinn had no one but Ethan, she ached to know her father, or at least know who he was. She also realized that whatever she uncovered might be better left buried, but she was ready to learn the truth, good or bad.

And here she was, holding a small cardboard box that could be the key.

She stood and put the box on the table beside the door. Ethan was expecting her to call and give him a rundown of her day. He wouldn't understand if she tried to tell him that she'd barely been able to function, much less figure out dinner. That she'd faked her way through the day, accomplishing almost nothing on her list, her entire system on full alert because of what she was about to do.

Ethan assumed she was still off because of her mother's death. He also knew that Quinn couldn't think of much else other than fulfilling her mom's wishes by taking her ashes to Maui and putting her to rest. He'd bought tickets and insisted she book the hotel reservations, declaring they'd make a vacation out of it. After Quinn memorialized her mother, of course.

They were set to leave in a month.

"It will help lift you out of this mood, Quinn," he'd said.

While he went on and on about the adventures Maui had to offer, Quinn was quiet, thinking of the moment when she'd have to leave her mother behind on the island. Traveling there was not going to be the mood-lifter he thought it was. Not for her.

There were things he didn't know, like the mystery of who her father was. It didn't feel right to tell him yet—she wanted this to stay between her and her mother for the time being. Quinn had a strong suspicion that the information her mom had been so intent on keeping to herself had probably poisoned her body, inviting the cancer in and allowing it to eat away until nothing was left but the shell of the woman Quinn had nearly worshipped. But even as her mother made her final will and testament, she'd not been able to bring herself to disclose the details of a story that could set her daughter free. *Why?*

She took a deep breath and readied herself, then picked up the phone.

Her fingers stiffened stubbornly, as though they didn't want to obey, but eventually there was a ring. Ethan picked up quickly.

"Hi," Quinn said.

"What's up?" he answered, his voice already hurrying her along. He was always running behind. "You headed for the gym?"

"No, I'm not. Listen, I need to talk to you." She felt her stomach clenching.

"Can it wait? I have a meeting in ten."

"No, it can't. I need to tell you now." *While I've got the courage,* she almost added.

"Hold on," he said. "Let me shut the door."

She could hear him bumping around, not sure what he was doing, but when he returned, her resolve weakened. Then she thought of her mother. A woman who deserved more than her daughter doing a quick dump of her ashes and then living it up around the island.

"I'm going to Maui alone," she blurted out.

"What do you mean?" He sounded confused.

"Ethan, I appreciate that you want to go and support me, but I need to do this by myself. I'm not looking forward to saying goodbye to the last of my mother. I want this to be a quiet and reflective time. A time to honor her in my own way."

"And you don't want me with you?" he said, his tone turning petulant.

"It's not that I don't want you with me. This just isn't the time to try to enjoy a vacation." *And I am hoping to find my real father.* That was another detail she wasn't ready to tell him.

"Quinn, I know you are still in a bad place, but you aren't thinking straight. We'll talk about this when I get home this weekend."

"No, we won't, Ethan. I've already canceled your flight. I'm serious about this. I'm sorry if it hurts you, but we'll plan to go again together after I've done what I need to do."

He sighed, long and frustrated.

"Sounds like I don't have a choice," he said. "I need to run."

He broke the connection, and she was left holding the phone to her ear, grasping it so tightly it made her fingers ache. When she lowered it, she was shaking.

Quinn liked routine and avoided drama at all costs. She felt safest in the cocoon she'd built around herself. But all that was about to be undone. Starting with a nondescript white box and a plane ticket, there was a secret with her name on it that Quinn meant to unravel.

Read More of True To Me here on Kindle, Paperback, or in Audio.

# About the Author

Photo © 2021 Stephanie Crump Photography

Writer, Rescuer, Wanderer

Kay Bratt is the powerhouse author behind over 35 internationally bestselling books that span genres from mystery and women's fiction to memoir and historical fiction. Her books are renowned for delivering an emotional wallop wrapped in gripping storylines. Her Hart's Ridge small-town mystery series earned her the coveted title of Amazon All Star Author and continues to be one of her most successful projects out of her more than two million books sold around the world.

Kay's literary works have sparked lively book club discussions wide-reaching, with her works translated into multiple languages, including German, Korean, Chinese, Hungarian, Czech, and Estonian.

Beyond her writing, Kay passionately dedicates herself to rescue missions, championing animal welfare as the former Director of Advocacy for Yorkie Rescue of the Carolinas. She considers herself a lifelong advocate for children, having volunteered extensively in a Chinese orphanage and supported nonprofit organizations like An Orphan's Wish (AOW), Pearl River Outreach, and Love Without Boundaries. In the USA, Kay served as a Court Appointed Special Advocate (CASA) for abused and neglected children in Georgia, as well as spearheaded numerous outreach programs for underprivileged kids in South Carolina.

As a wanderlust-driven soul, Kay has called nearly three dozen different homes on two continents her own. Her globe-trotting adventures have taken her to captivating destinations across Mexico, Thailand, Malaysia, China, the Philippines, Central America, the Bahamas, and Australia. Today, she and her soulmate of 30+ years find their sanctuary by the serene banks of Lake Hartwell in Georgia, USA.

Described as southern, spicy, and a touch sassy, Kay loves to share her life's antics with the Bratt Pack on social media. Follow her on Facebook, Twitter, and Instagram to join the fun and buckle up for the ride of a lifetime. Explore her popular catalog of published works at Kay Bratt Dot-Com and never miss a new release (or her latest Bratt Pack drama) by signing up for her monthly email newsletter. For more information, visit www.kaybratt.com.